Gabriel barged into the room, keeping Natalie behind him…

It took a moment to process what he was seeing. The escaped convict he'd seen on the news reports stood at the foot of the bed, his hands clenched into fists, his eyes boring into Natalie.

Gabriel didn't know exactly how she knew this man or what was transpiring between them now. He only knew that Natalie was scared to death this man came to the lodge looking for her.

Well, he knew one other thing. He knew that he couldn't let that happen.

Tensing his muscles, he took two steps toward the escaped prisoner. He never even saw the convict's brother, John, come from behind the open door and close the distance between them fast.

"Gabriel! Watch out!" Natalie shouted.

Gabriel turned just in time to see John rear back and swing. He tried to duck and block, but he was too late. The room lit up bright white, and then everything went black…

Jennifer Brown is the award-winning author of young adult and middle-grade novels, including *Perfect Escape*, *Thousand Words*, *Torn Away* and the Shade Me series. Her acclaimed debut novel, *Hate List*, was selected as an ALA Best Book for Young Adults, a *VOYA* "Perfect Ten" and a *School Library Journal* Best Book of the Year, and her novel *Bitter End* was a 2012 YALSA Best Fiction for Young Adults. Her debut middle-grade novel, *Life on Mars*, was the winner of the 2017 William Allen White Children's Book Award.

Jennifer is also the nationally bestselling author of several women's fiction novels under the pseudonym Jennifer Scott. She lives in Kansas City, Missouri. Visit her at jenniferbrownauthor.com.

Books by Jennifer Brown

Love Inspired Inspirational Mountain Rescue

Rescue on the Ridge
Peril at the Peak

Visit the Author Profile page at LoveInspired.com.

Hunted at the Hideaway

JENNIFER BROWN

LOVE INSPIRED
INSPIRATIONAL ROMANCE

LOVE INSPIRED®

INSPIRATIONAL ROMANCE

Recycling programs
for this product may
not exist in your area.

ISBN-13: 978-1-335-46836-9

Hunted at the Hideaway

Copyright © 2023 by Jennifer Brown

For questions and comments about the quality of this book, please contact us
at CustomerService@Harlequin.com.

Love Inspired
22 Adelaide St. West, 41st Floor
Toronto, Ontario M5H 4E3, Canada
www.LoveInspired.com

Printed in U.S.A.

Fear thou not; for I am with thee: be not dismayed;
for I am thy God: I will strengthen thee;
yea, I will help thee; yea, I will uphold thee
with the right hand of my righteousness.
—*Isaiah* 41:10

For Scott

Acknowledgments

In many ways, the writing process is a game of cat and mouse. The story idea is out there somewhere, hiding in this corner or that shadow, slipping away when you think you've got it trapped, jumping out at you at the least convenient moment possible, sometimes scaring you with its inevitability. Natalie and Gabriel have each other as they traverse the dark hallways of the Snowed Inn Hideaway; I've got the following people to help me chase down my story.

Thank you to my agent, Cori Deyoe, for being my right hand, my stability, my optimism and my storyboard. I would face the bad guys to save you any day.

Thank you to the Love Inspired team for your diligent work in making *Hunted at the Hideaway* the best it could possibly be. Special thanks to Greg Stephenson for the copyediting work, to Melissa Kealoha for the cover design and especially to my editor, Johanna Raisanen, for your keen eye, your helpful suggestions and for always pointing out the things that work. Your positivity and encouragement are inspiring.

Thank you to my family. You all are everything.

And, finally, thank You to God, for always being there to hold me up, even in the darkest of hallways and coldest of storms.

Prologue

"This is it," Maeve said, squeezing Natalie's hand as they walked briskly through the lobby of the courthouse. The prosecutor's spiral curls sprang with each clack of her high heels, making Natalie's tentative, shuffling steps seem all the more pronounced. Her ribs ached with every intake of breath, but it had been that way for so long, she hardly even noticed it anymore. It seemed impossible that she'd never even heard of Maeve Shoals before last year. Their lives had become so intertwined. Maeve was determined to put Jed Grunder away for a long, long time. And Natalie, his victim, was even more determined to help her. "This is what we've worked for. Are you okay?"

Natalie nodded, quick, jerky movements, as she desperately tried to just remember to breathe: *in and out, in and out, slower, slower...*

Maeve didn't look convinced. "You don't have to go in there. I can let you know after it's over, if you'd like. You've already done the most important part."

"I want to be in there to hear it," Natalie said.

Maeve studied Natalie with the same ferocity that she aimed at everything. Truth be told, Natalie wished she was more like Maeve Shoals, fearless and self-assured. "Okay. But if they find him not guilty… Well, you already know."

Natalie's lips felt extremely dry. "Do you think they will? You said this was a good sign, them coming back so quickly. You said we should be hopeful."

Maeve shook her head, closing her eyes as if to dismiss the words before Natalie could even get them all the way out. When she reopened them, her intense gaze had softened. "I don't think they will. But there's always a chance. And it could be hard for you to see him get released."

Hard wouldn't even begin to describe it. It would be impossible. Natalie couldn't even think about it without feeling a familiar crush deep inside her chest.

"I'm sure. I'm going in," she said, squeezing the attorney's hand before letting it go and walking into the courtroom behind her.

God, I need to lean on you right now. Please be my strength.

Natalie had some difficulty with the idea of praying to the God who let this horrible thing happen to her; this prayer was going through the motions. A spiritual insurance policy.

It felt like she'd barely sat down before the judge arrived and got right down to business. Suddenly, she was sure that she was too unfocused and unprepared for this. It was all happening too quickly.

The judge was talking, and Maeve, sitting directly in front of Natalie, was nodding. Natalie focused on the tiny spirals at the nape of Maeve's neck—similar to her own—doing everything she could not to look at Jed Grunder, who stood next to his attorney, his chin held high and defiant. Natalie's hands shook. It had been a very long road. Recovery, research and a dogged resolve to see Jed Grunder behind bars if it was the last thing she did. And sometimes she felt as if it might be the last thing she did.

Words bounced off of her, as if the judge were speaking in a whisper, in another language, behind a closed door. She couldn't hear, and what she could hear, she couldn't understand. Her brain was too busy sorting through images: standing at her apartment door, smiling as Jed Grunder approached her, and then a white flash of pain that disoriented her, spinning walls as she tumbled down the stairs, Jed's boot as it came at her again and again… Her ears began ringing, as they always did when these unbidden memories washed over her. She squeezed her eyes tight and repeated the Lord's Prayer, a calming tactic she'd learned as a child.

There was a muffled whoop, and Natalie sensed movement around her. Maeve was now leaning over the rail that separated them and was holding her arms out for a hug. She was smiling. Natalie's ears were still ringing, but sound had begun to come into focus. Maeve's mouth was moving, her words sounding as if she were speaking from the bottom of a lake.

"What?" Natalie asked.

"I said, we did it!" Maeve repeated. "We got him."

Natalie blinked in slow motion, allowing herself to be hugged, feeling herself nodding, Maeve's assistant simultaneously patting her on the back, as if she'd just won a race. And maybe in some ways she had. It certainly felt like a marathon most days. The courtroom swam back into focus, and over Maeve's shoulder, Natalie accidentally let her eyes wander to Jed Grunder, who was caught up in his own wave of motion, his attorneys on either side of him hurriedly speaking promises, a bailiff pulling on the crook of his arm.

"We'll fix this, Jed! We'll fix it," Jed's brother, John, shouted from across the room. "It's okay. It's temporary."

But Jed didn't appear to notice any of the things that were happening around him. He had a laser-sharp focus on Natalie.

It might have been less jarring had his face been angry. But it was stony, emotionless, as if he were taking everything in as fact that he would store to deal with later. And then, even worse, one side of his mouth turned up into a grin, sending shock waves of fear through Natalie.

Jed's attorneys turned and began packing up their papers, and the bailiff tugged harder on Jed's arm, forcing him to walk. He followed, his eyes never leaving Natalie's, until, at the last moment, just before he turned away, he mouthed two words at her.

You're dead.

Chapter One

Natalie Marlowe wasn't a big TV-watcher to begin with, and as owner of the Snowed Inn Hideaway, she was simply too busy to pay attention to the goings-on in the world at the bottom of the mountain. The news didn't often affect her, anyway. Time was different in her remote area of Bighorn. Less urgent. Less noisy. That was why she'd chosen it. Her life was sheets and towels, broken skis and squeaky lift chairs, check-ins and checkouts, not politics and bickering and bad days. And she liked it that way.

But, on occasion, a newsworthy event would find its way onto the little TV in the Hideaway's dining room and force Natalie's attention. Guests would ask for the volume to be turned up, and they would eat their French toast and scrambled eggs with their eyes glued to the screen, their plans on the slopes temporarily forgotten.

Today was one of those occasions. And as guests finished their breakfasts and made their way to the desk to change their reservations—*sorry, so sorry, we hate to cut our vacation short, but we really should get back, given the forecast*—Natalie became more and more aware of a giant storm headed their way. For ski resort owners, snow was rarely bad news. But huge storms that chased guests off the mountain, causing them to cut their vacations short, certainly weren't the best news in the world.

This incoming storm wouldn't be the biggest she'd ever seen at the Hideaway. She'd been there the winter that the wind was so swift, she lost a lift bench right off the line, and they literally had to wait for a thaw before they could open the front door. But there was no doubt, this storm was going to be a doozy. Ice, then snow—a lot of it—then more ice. Wind, cold. The whole shebang. She and her right-hand employee, Cora, started making plans to hunker down and wait it out. Groceries were bought, firewood was chopped, library books were procured.

Cora, a sturdy woman in her mid-forties, had begun working at the Hideaway only a week or so after Natalie appeared, barely out of her teens. Together, they learned the ropes of lodge management under the tutelage of a tough widowed Highlander named Ruth. The three of them had run the Hideaway together, but Ruth had taken a particular shine to Natalie, teaching her everything about handling a ski lodge. When Ruth died, Natalie was mortified to find that Ruth had left the Hideaway to her rather than to Cora, but Cora waved it away, saying Natalie was the natural-born leader, and Ruth always knew what she was doing, so why would that change now. Natalie had reluctantly taken the reins, and she and Cora became a single lodge management unit. Cora knew every bit of what Natalie knew, and then some. But, most importantly, Cora knew Natalie, and that was huge. Natalie relied on Cora on a daily—sometimes hourly—basis.

Breakfast was over, and the little dining room was empty. Natalie had finished wiping the last table, and Kim, their kitchen manager, had washed the dishes and headed home until after the storm passed. Natalie turned off the little TV and tossed another log onto the fire. It was quiet in the lodge.

She sidled up to Cora, who was running the front desk.

"All done with checkouts?" Natalie asked.

Cora nodded. "Most everyone is upstairs packing. Cookies are in the oven." She checked her watch. "Should be done in eight minutes. I'll have them on a plate by the front door before the first car is loaded."

"Well, since you have everything under control here, I'm going to do a little check on our outside friends."

"Say hello for me."

Natalie smirked, grabbed a pair of gloves and a scarf out of the box in the coat closet and put them on while she walked to the front door. She wound her arms through the sleeves of her coat, grabbed a bag of peanuts and a small bucket of birdseed off the top shelf of the closet and stepped outside.

The lodge wasn't a maze of cabins and gift shops

like some of those other sprawling ski resorts but was more of a large, yet still cozy, bed-and-breakfast. Just three floors—a main floor front desk and gathering space, with two floors containing twenty-five guest rooms stacked on top. No swimming pool, no hot tub, no elevators. Just a couple of staircases and two long, U-shaped hallways. Simple meals were prepared in the employee kitchen on the main floor, and room service was secreted up a back employee stairwell that bookended the hallways. Outside was a quick, downhill walk to the lift, which ran guests right up to an easy, scenic slope. It wasn't a place to show off or throw big, raucous parties, but rather a place to lie back, enjoy gathering with family and new friends and commune with the mountain rather than conquer it.

And it was home for both Natalie and Cora. And had been for nearly six years now. Cora was all about the intimate, friendly setting, and Natalie loved the retro, snow bunny vibe, as well as the seclusion.

The weather was still mild, but the wind was picking up, and Natalie could smell snow on the air. The sky was white, as if loaded and ready to burst. She crunched through the snow that was already on the ground—the hard-packed stuff that really never went away—pausing to pick up a discarded candy wrapper that had wound itself around the front porch rail. She rounded the porch and headed for the bird and squirrel feeders.

It was quiet back there. Too quiet.

She felt a shiver run down her spine. For the past

several days, she couldn't shake the feeling of being watched. She whipped around, squinting into the woods, scanning for telltale signs of an outsider. Footprints, a scent of cologne on the air, anything that she might have missed years ago, before Jed Grunder attacked her. But, as always, there was nothing. It was just a feeling, and she was creeping herself out needlessly. Surely, it was the heaviness of the snow in the upper atmosphere that she was picking up on.

Or…she *was* being watched. By a beady-eyed little friend.

"Hello, Felix," she said as she poured a mound of peanuts onto the squirrel feeder; the dried corn cob she'd just placed there the day before was chewed to smithereens. As if he'd only been waiting for his invitation, Felix the squirrel scurried along the branch above Natalie until he was in her view. "You scared me, sir. You don't have to wait for an invitation, you know." She poured the peanuts into the feeder. He began snatching them up before Natalie had even turned her back, making her giggle. "Make sure you get plenty. There's a storm coming. Take some home to your family."

There was a sudden movement behind her—a thump on the ground, a rustle of foliage. She gasped, her hand going to her heart as she spun to face the noise. It seemed to be coming from a spruce tree about twenty feet away. The branches, which had at first appeared to be swaying in the wind, were now jostling.

There was someone in there, in the space where the branches hid the trunk.

The jostling turned into a shiver, and then a nose popped out, followed by a little muzzle and two big eyes.

Her hand still on her heart, Natalie began to giggle again. Not a someone—a some*thing*. A deer.

"Well, hello, little one. I didn't even see you," she said. "I hope I didn't disturb you. I didn't realize you had a home inside there. I'll bring you some apples later, how about that?"

The deer stood stock-still, seemingly listening to her, and then darted back under the cover of the low spruce tree branches.

Natalie moved to the bird feeders, filling each one, and checked the water level on the heated birdbaths. Satisfied that everything was shipshape, she wandered back to the lodge, set the empty bucket and bag on the porch rail and turned to survey the rest of the grounds.

The wind blew, bringing with it a rhythmic thumping sound. Instantly, her heart ramped up, and her muscles tensed. She held her breath without realizing it. The same shivers that had raised the hairs on the back of her neck had returned, only this time running down the length of her arms. Again, she had a sense of not being alone out here, and it made her jumpy.

She scanned until she found the source of the banging: the lift terminal. The door had been left open and was flapping in the wind, against the side of the terminal.

She sighed. "Oh, Jordan."

Sweet, absent-minded Jordan, the college student

she'd hired to run the lift during the weekends, was forever leaving the lift station unlocked. Seemed like every other day he was standing in front of her, twisting his beanie in his hands, saying, *My bad, Miss Marlowe, I was daydreaming, I guess*, or, *I was late to dinner and my mom was blowing up my phone*, or, *I was thinking about my homework*. The tops of his cheeks always got red, making his freckles stand out. She found it so endearing, she could hardly stay mad at him. He was a great kid; leaving a door unlocked way up here was not the worst thing in the world.

"You could at least close the door, though," she said aloud. Her lift was old, and she constantly worried about it breaking down. The last thing she needed was someone—or something—getting inside the terminal and helping the process along.

She traipsed over and shut the door, making a mental note that she would need to grab her key inside and lock it up later, after one more stop.

She walked across the lift pass and into the tree line on the other side and paused. She was so jumpy today, maybe it wasn't an ideal day for going into the woods. *Don't be ridiculous, Natalie, you're just getting into your own head,* she told herself and then took a long inhale.

There was a different smell to the snow inside the trees. Something cleaner and greener. To Natalie, maybe the most comforting scent in the world. She closed her eyes and let her shoulders relax. This was the reason she came to Bighorn. For silence, solitude.

Don't forget for fear, her brain tried to supply, but

she batted that thought away. Not fear. Just a shifting of priorities. *Don't forget robberies and vicious attacks that leave you lying at the bottom of a stairway with your life floating away from you. That also brought you up here.*

Right on cue, the scar high up on the side of her head began aching—something she knew to be psychosomatic, but all these years later, she still had yet to figure out how to chase away. It wouldn't be long before she'd feel phantom pain in her ribs, her back, all of the places where Jed Grunder had literally kicked her while she was down.

Okay, so maybe she was at Bighorn a little bit out of fear. At first. But she loved it here. The fear was long gone.

She opened her eyes and looked up at the sky through the leaves, appreciating the designs and patterns in dark against light. In two days, those leaves would be heavy with snow, dipping down to let powdery little puffs fall to the ground. She would be able to put her hand on a trunk, give a tree a good shake, and live inside a miniblizzard if she wanted to— something that often delighted young guests. But the guests were all headed down the mountain. It would be a personal miniblizzard, which wasn't necessarily a bad thing.

She pushed through the woods, knowing exactly where to step, what deceptive footholds to avoid, where a patch of pine needles was perennially slippery, where an ankle-twisting hole was buried under snow and leaves. She'd walked the route so many times, she'd forged a little path there, but one only she could recognize as a path. Not that anyone else had ever even tried to wander back here.

Except…someone had. Recently. There were footsteps in the muddy slush. They seemed to lead all different directions. There was something about the prints that made her uneasy. Maybe it was the way they looped toward the edge of the tree line and dipped back inside again. Like someone had been watching the lodge.

She was being silly, of course. It was probably just a curious guest, stepping into the forest for a look-see but afraid of wandering too far in.

The trees opened up, growing sparse enough that she could see her destination. She paused, frowning. Someone was already there, sitting in her spot on her ledge. For a moment, her brain went all directions at once, not the least of which was a vague feeling of satisfaction that she was right in her suspicion that someone besides herself was out here. Her gut instinct wasn't always wrong. It was really only wrong once; that one time just happened to be terribly wrong and terribly tragic.

She shifted, turning back toward the way she'd come, her foot crunching against a dead branch that had fallen on top of the snow.

"Hello?" The man sitting on the ledge turned to peer into the woods.

Natalie winced. Now she had no choice but to interact. "Hi," she called back, putting on her Professional Voice. "I didn't realize there was anyone out here. I'll go."

"No, stay," the man said. "There's room for both of us. Is it okay for me…? I'm sorry, are guests allowed to…? I followed a path in the snow, and it led me directly here. Am I breaking some sort of rule or something being out here?"

Only unspoken ones. "Not at all. We want you to feel free to enjoy the grounds. I'll go and give you privacy."

The figure moved, hopping to his feet, and coming closer to the woods. Her heart tried to leap around in her throat—a lingering response she figured she would always have at the sight or sound of a man approaching her when she was alone. He took a few steps into the trees, and she could see he was definitely one of her guests. The man from room 204. Gabriel Neesom. Blond hair, blue eyes, muscular and agile. He'd been at the Hideaway for nearly a week and seemed to be contemplating something, working out a problem. He had been a relatively unassuming guest—never demanding anything—but had caught Natalie's attention, even though after what had happened with Jed Grunder, she was set against ever letting any man catch her attention as long as she lived. She was in the middle of nowhere for a reason, after all, and all the Gabriel Neesoms in the world couldn't override that reason.

Still, he was nice.

He got close enough for Natalie to see his smile, which was genuine and bright and, at the moment, filled with playful wonder. "I didn't mean to be taking anyone's space. It's just so beautiful here. I can go."

Natalie was shocked to find herself taking two tentative steps forward. "It's not my space. Well, I mean, I'm usually the only one who knows it's here, but it's not mine. It's—"

"God's," they both said at the same time.

His smile grew wider and he pointed at her. "Yes! Exactly! There's an eagle's nest, have you seen it?"

She nodded. "Henrietta's."

He cocked his head to the side, quizzical. "Henrietta?"

She could feel her cheeks get warm and wondered if they were growing red just like Jordan's tended to do. "I name the regulars," she said. "I've got a squirrel—Felix. A white-tail deer family that comes around—Marge, and her two fawns, Otto and Victor. And…" She gestured toward the nest that she couldn't see from her current vantage point but had been watching for so long she knew its exact location. "And that's Henrietta, the bald eagle mama." There were more, of course, but the longer she talked, the shier she became. She didn't want to be the weird lodge owner who talked to animals like they were people. Cora knew that Natalie talked to them, but even she didn't know Natalie had named them.

But Gabriel didn't seem in the least bit bothered by this. His grin grew into a full-on smile. Something about that smile made Natalie comfortable, and she took a few more steps toward him without even realizing it.

"Sometimes," she said, pointing into the break between some trees below, "if you look in that direction, you'll catch a glimpse of a couple of moose that hang out down there. They've never come up here, but occasionally they'll pop out of the trees and we'll watch each other for a while."

"So you hang out here a lot," Gabriel said.

Natalie nodded. "Just about every day. I think of it as my pondering ledge."

"That's exactly what I was doing here."

As a general rule, Natalie trusted nothing, so she couldn't explain what made her take those last few steps through the trees. There was something about Gabriel Neesom that was instantly comfortable. Familiar, not as if she knew him, but as if she could see herself in him. *He could shove you right off of this ledge,* her brain nagged, but she took those steps anyway, until she was stepping out onto the ledge next to him, the entire world opening up in front of her.

This was the view that made her decide to keep the old ski lodge exactly the way it had been when Ruth was still alive. Any place with a view like this was special. Untouchable. She could be alone without feeling alone. Be small without feeling vulnerable. It was as if the world hummed around her up here, pushing her further away from pain. She would have thought she'd be disappointed that someone else had found it. But, surprisingly, she wasn't. She was kind of…excited to share.

It was probably due to the look of wonder on his

face as he scanned the tops of the pine, fir and spruce trees below, right along with her.

She pointed. "In the spring, that little lake draws all sorts of animals. I've seen black bear cubs playing in the water. So cute. I watched them for hours. And over there—" she pointed in a different direction "—I've seen coyote pups. I don't really love the idea of coyotes coming around the lodge, but watching the pups tumble around is pretty fun. As long as they stay down there. Same with mountain lions."

Gabriel looked alarmed. "Mountain lions?"

She waved him away. "I've had one or two approach the cabin, and one time a cub even tried to get in. But they pretty much stay to themselves. They only attack if they feel threatened or are starving or something's wrong."

Gabriel crouched, and then sat, his legs crossed. "I don't know how you get any work done. I would sit here all day if I could," he said. "When you're skiing, it's like you're part of the mountain, kind of like you're one with it, and that's pretty great. But sitting here is a whole different feeling. Like you're part of something much, much bigger. Like you don't always have to be the one in charge. There's freedom in that." He offered her a shrug. "Maybe I'm overthinking things. I do that. It's kind of why I'm here to begin with. To overthink."

Natalie felt an urge to lower herself to the ground next to him, but something—a familiar prickle up her spine—kept her from doing so. "It's why I'm here, too," she said. "The being in charge part, not the overthinking part. I can do that anywhere. I'm talented that way. Although I suppose this is my favorite spot and where I do it most often."

Gabriel ducked his head and laughed, eliciting a chuckle out of Natalie that felt good and easy. He offered her a handshake. "Well, welcome to the Overthinkers Club," he said. "I'm Gabriel, the founder and head overthinker."

And just like that, the good and easy feeling vanished. When she looked at his outstretched hand, all Natalie could think of was him pulling her over the ledge and sending her to a painful, tumbling death, just as Jed Grunder had sent her tumbling down the stairs of her apartment. Her breath caught, and it must have shown on her face, because his smile faded and he lowered his hand.

"I mean…" he said, but he didn't seem to know how to finish.

Now the heat in Natalie's cheeks felt much more uncomfortable. Embarrassing. Urgent. "No, it's just…" The wind gusted, whisking her words away, and she wished it would carry her away, too. Carry her away from this conversation but also from the past that ruined conversations like these for her. She forced a smile, coaxed her shoulders to relax. "I highly recommend this as the best thinking spot in the world. Or… you know…overthinking spot."

But the joke had already been ruined. He was intuitive. Natalie felt a little bit seen by him and found that she didn't entirely hate the idea. He cleared his throat and turned to gaze at the valley below again. "How is it for decision-making?" he asked.

"I've made a few."

He nodded. "Good. I have a few to make. Well, one big one that would set off an avalanche of little ones."

Natalie exaggerated a wince. "We don't like that word around here."

"Decisions?"

"Avalanche."

"Ah," he said, amusement creeping back in like a shy child at a party. "That makes total sense." There was a beat, and then, "If you don't mind my asking... what did you do before you did this?" He gestured at the mountain, as if to indicate the entire mountain itself.

"I've been on the mountain for quite a while," she said. "I don't even remember what life was like before." *Lie, lie, lie.*

"Ah, so you've always wanted to do this."

Not always, she thought, but then she realized she couldn't exactly remember what she might have wanted before she left the city. She'd been so young. If she couldn't remember any other dreams, did that mean that technically this was what she always wanted? She wasn't sure.

But if she was happy, did it really matter? She guessed not. It may not have been her dream before, but it had become her dream now.

She dodged the question. "I love it here, yes."

"What's not to love?" he said, peering out into the valley again.

"Does this mean you're staying through the storm?" she asked. "You haven't changed your reservations."

"I'm not afraid of a little snow."

"It won't be a little."

"I'm not afraid of a lot of snow, either," he said. "Being snowed in might be just what I need. Might clear my head, help me make my decision. Or, you know, it might freeze me into a Gabe-sicle. And then my big decisions won't matter anymore. You can just park my frozen self on this ledge, and I will spend eternity watching Henrietta."

Gabriel Neesom was funny. She had to admit—she was a little bit happy he'd be sticking around. Of the sides of her that warred against each other—the side that said to open herself up versus the side that said to protect herself at all costs—she found herself being pulled to the side that included spending more time with him.

"Well, Henrietta does put on quite a show," Natalie said. "But we have plenty of firewood to keep anyone from becoming a human Popsicle. We would probably just park you there to thaw."

"Glad to know I'm in good hands," he said.

"Speaking of firewood," Natalie said. "I should probably get back to the lodge. Make sure we've got plenty of it inside and ready to go. Enjoy your decision-making."

"Hmm," he said, frowning off at the frozen lake, where, in the spring, bears would frolic as if there was never a big decision to be made in this world.

Natalie made her way back through the woods, moving quickly, silently berating herself for letting a feeling of connection creep in and cause her to share with Gabriel Neesom. As if she hadn't already learned what sharing with a man you didn't really know could lead to.

By the time she got back to the lodge and was checking the woodpile, she'd already convinced herself that she would just have to steer clear of personal sharing with Gabriel Neesom from here on out. Keep things friendly, but professional.

Even if part of her doubted that was going to be possible.

It wasn't until she was about to head in that something he said totally dawned on her: *I followed a path in the snow, and it led me directly here.*

If Gabriel hadn't been the one making the wandering footprints in the snow...who had?

By the next morning, most of the other guests were already gone, but Gabriel didn't really mind. More French toast for him. He'd quickly become addicted to the sweet breakfast and was tucked into a plate, just as he'd been doing every morning, ignoring the weather channel looping the radar as he *tap-tap-tapped* away on his laptop, creating a pros-and-cons list.

Pro: Change needed.
Pro: No more surprises.
Con: Expensive.

He'd been a private investigator for the past ten years. He was good at it. He had a knack for being unseen, for being able to fade into the shadows, but also for being calm in the face of danger, for being unafraid to be places where he really shouldn't have been and for taking the occasional licking, wiping away the blood and the bruises, and getting back out there again.

Until the blow that just hit too hard. His heart hadn't been into investigation since. Hadn't been into much of anything.

It was a year ago. He'd decided to follow Liane, the girl he'd been dating since college, just for one day. He'd had a good reason. He'd bought an engagement ring and was trying to think of the best way to surprise her with it. He'd wanted the perfect proposal and had hoped trailing her for a day would inspire him.

Instead, he was the one who was surprised. And not at all in a good way.

"Warm cookie?" He was ripped out of his sour memory by a plate nudging into his field of vision.

He looked up, his fingers paused over his keyboard, and grinned. Natalie stood next to his table holding a tray of cookies. There was something comforting about Natalie. Something that just clicked between them. She was beautiful in a wild, untamed sort of way. Her dark hair sprung out in loose curls every which way, and she continually brushed it out of her face, tucked it behind her ears. Her eyes, the hue of the sky when they were outside, were somehow also the color of the trees when they were inside.

But she definitely had painful memories of her own. Memories that he had a feeling she wouldn't easily share with anyone. He'd had a distinct impression that they'd been talking around it on the ledge the day before. He'd wanted her to stay, even if they only sat together in silence and watched the scenery. Even if they only overthought, side by side.

"Would you like a warm cookie?" she repeated, wiggling the tray a little.

"I'm going to need to go on a diet after leaving this place. I've surely eaten a whole loaf of French toast by now."

"Well, you're going to love these, then. They're both Granny's recipes." She pressed the tray in a little closer. "You can never go wrong with Granny."

He laughed, ducking his head just a little. "If I must…" He took two cookies, bit into one and groaned approvingly. "Your grandma knows her way around a kitchen."

"*Knew* her way around a kitchen," Natalie corrected. "She passed when I was twelve. But I'd already learned so much from her, I decided to continue to make her recipes so I wouldn't forget them. Sort of like…her legacy, I guess? It's comforting to me. And she would love the idea of sharing her prized butterscotch chocolate chip cookies with guests."

"What an excellent legacy to leave behind," he said, taking another bite. "You are doing her justice, and I'm honored to be the recipient."

He thought he saw Natalie blush and then purposefully collect herself. This was what he'd noticed about her from the beginning—she seemed to always be at war with herself, wanting to reach out, and then pulling back in again, a turtle afraid to come out of its shell. He would be lying if he said he didn't know a little something about hiding, as well.

"Normally, they're a goodbye gift for our guests, but I kind of think you're owed a gift for staying while everyone else is checking out. Still not worried about the storm?"

He gestured toward his computer. "I've got something to keep me occupied. I'm all good."

"The power lines aren't the best up here," she said. "Occasionally we lose it, if the wind's strong enough."

"I'll read by the fire. So much cozier than all that slush down in the valley."

"Honestly, they'll probably get more snow down there than we do up here, so all of the people who left this morning are headed right for it."

"Ah, well...see, I'm exactly where I need to be, then," he said. "Besides, I'm not the only one staying." He gestured to the man sitting across the room, who was bent over a laptop of his own. Natalie frowned as she followed Gabriel's gaze, confirming the strange feeling of mistrust that he'd gotten every time he was around the man. "Is something wrong?"

"What? No." She gave a nervous laugh. "There's just something familiar about him. I haven't been myself the past couple days. It's probably the storm putting me on edge. I'm sure he's just reminding me of someone."

"Maybe he's been here before?" Gabriel suggested.

"Maybe," Natalie agreed. She nodded and offered a weak smile. "Yes, that's probably it. Anyway, you're welcome to more cookies anytime. Just ask. And let me know if you need anything."

"Just a good, old-fashioned snowstorm to help me focus," he said, gesturing to his keyboard. He took another bite of cookie.

Con: I can't get Granny's cookies if I'm stuck in law school.

"Well, prepare to focus. We've definitely got one of those coming our way." She left, and it was just Gabriel and his thoughts again. And a whole lot of sugar. He found himself sneaking glances at the other man in the dining room.

Natalie definitely wasn't the only one suspicious of him. Gabriel had been keeping an eye on him basically from the moment he checked in. The man set every warning bell ringing in Gabriel's head. He had come to trust that warning bell. And now, seeing Natalie's reaction, he trusted it even more.

"Everything taste okay?" The other woman who worked at the Hideaway—Cora—was gesturing toward Gabriel's plate.

"Oh, yes. Thank you."

Like Natalie had just done a moment ago, Cora followed Gabriel's gaze to the man, whose full plate sat on the edge of his table, untouched. "He never eats what he orders," she whispered. "It's a bit strange. He hasn't left the Hideaway, so if he's not eating here…"

"His room?" Gabriel supplied.

She shrugged. "I have no idea. He also has never

taken the Do Not Disturb sign off of his door, so I haven't gotten in there to clean. But he has to be eating in there, right? He can't just be…starving. He's been here for three days. I really would like to get the dishes and trash out of that room, if that's the case."

"He doesn't know what he's missing out on. This French toast…" Gabriel stabbed a cut piece with his fork and held it in the air appreciatively before popping it into his mouth.

"But why order it if he isn't going to eat it?" Cora asked, then shook her head, seemingly to shake herself out of her thought. "You know what? I shouldn't be saying anything. I never talk about the guests. I don't know why I'm laying that on you."

He offered a grin. "I have one of those faces," he said. "It's an invitation face. People tell me things all the time. In the line at the market, in the lobby at the car dealership, everywhere. I should have been a therapist."

"Or a pastor," Cora said.

Gabriel thought of his pastor, who was the reason he was at the Hideaway to begin with, having encouraged him to get away for a bit to wrestle with his big decision. *You'll be surprised how much better you can hear God when you get away from all of the other noise*, Pastor Roy had said, sitting across from Gabriel at the Wednesday fellowship dinner. Gabriel had instantly known the man was right. He was hearing a lot of noise. A lot of differing internal voices telling him what the right thing was and what the wrong thing was and what about this thing or that thing and had he ever considered this thing over here?

His first day at the Hideaway, he'd gone for a hike and discovered the small ledge that Natalie had found him on. It was hidden from the rest of the resort by some trees, and he didn't even know how he found it—it was almost like it had called to him. When he stepped out onto the ledge, the entire world had opened up in front of him. God's beauty and glory. Rolling mountains as far as the eye could see. Trees and boulders and birds swooping in and out of view. Plump clouds bobbing along on a sky that was so blue he could almost feel it rather than see it.

And there it was. The silence that he needed. He'd sat on the ground and closed his eyes, tipping his face to the sun.

What should I do? he'd prayed. *Show me my path.*

He couldn't ignore how Natalie had appeared on that very ledge days later, as if she herself was the path. But once upon a time he'd thought Liane was his path, so he definitely couldn't trust thoughts like those.

"*Are* you a pastor?" Cora asked. "You don't have to answer that. I'm just being nosy now."

"It's okay. Definitely not a pastor. Private investigator," he said. "For now, anyway."

"Ah," she said. "So you're saving the world, one injustice at a time?"

He smiled. "Something like that. If the cons outweigh the pros."

"I don't understand."

He gestured to his computer screen. "I'm thinking of leaving investigation and going back to school. Law school. Which is a big decision. I've been writing a pros-and-cons list, but it's not really helping."

"Hmm..." Cora tapped her chin. "Are you good at private investigation?"

"I think I am."

"Do you like it?"

"I don't know. Sometimes you discover things you were never meant to witness. You know what I mean?"

There was a jangle of music on the TV that distracted both of them, and the words "Breaking News" spun and tumbled onto the screen. For what seemed like the first time in days, the camera tore away from the meteorologist, a mug shot filling the screen instead, the words "Fugitive Prisoner" appearing beneath it.

Cora pointed. "That's the guy who broke out of prison. They can't find him. Maybe you should track him. Can you imagine? You'd be a hero."

Gabriel didn't need to be anyone's hero; he just needed to make up his mind.

The man on the other side of the dining room stood and stretched, then shut his computer and pushed his chair into the table. He glanced at the TV, picked up his computer and his full plate and skulked out of the room. There was something there. Gabriel could feel it. Cora could feel it. And somehow he knew that Natalie could feel it, too.

Chapter Two

Natalie dumped the last load of clean towels onto a table and sank down into a chair next to Cora. She was exhausted after cleaning all of the emptied rooms. Having everyone leave at once meant turning them all at once, and it was tiring to say the least. Natalie picked a towel off the top of the pile and began folding. Cora absently nibbled a cookie while her eyes stayed glued to the TV.

"What more could they possibly have to say about the weather?" Natalie wondered aloud. "It's snow. It's not like we've never seen it before."

Cora shook her head. "It's not the storm they're talking about. It's that guy. The one who escaped from the penitentiary. He's been out for over a day, and they still have no idea where he could be. They think he's probably trying to run across the border, but the storm may drive him to try to take shelter. They're telling people to make sure all doors and windows are locked, just in case. Can you imagine? You're sitting in your house, eating dinner, watching TV, and all of a sudden, the guy on the TV is standing in your living room? Terrifying."

Natalie picked up and folded another towel, and then another. She shook her head. "That's why you shouldn't watch TV."

"I suppose you're right," Cora said. "But…someone could sneak in through the back door, go through the kitchen and right up the back stairs. They could be lurking in our lodge at this very minute. Just waiting. We would never know. I think about that all the time."

Natalie laughed and waved a towel at Cora. "You listen to too many true crime podcasts. The penitentiary is hours from here. What would he want to do with this place? We're not exactly on the way to… anything. Not even the border. He's on foot. He's not going to come up here. And, besides, if he did come here, you would definitely know. With all the checkouts, you've been in and out of every room in this B&B over the past two days. Surely you would have noticed a fugitive hiding behind a shower curtain. And we keep the back door locked anyway."

"Not always. Sometimes Jordan leaves it unlocked. Sometimes you or I go out for firewood and our hands are full and we forget and leave it unlocked."

"We're a hotel. Our front door is always unlocked. It sort of has to be."

"Does it, though?" Cora asked. "They're saying to lock up everything. And all of our guests have left, so what does it matter?"

"Not all of them," Natalie said. "Mr. Davis is still

checked in. He stepped out a while ago and I haven't seen him come back yet. Hopefully he beats the storm."

"That reminds me," Cora said, lowering her voice. "The other guest... Gabriel, I think?"

"Mmm-hmm, Gabriel Neesom."

"Yeah, him. I saw him chatting up Mr. Davis earlier, and Mr. Davis wasn't having it. Was totally rude to him. So I asked him about it, and he said he's certain that Mr. Davis is using an alias. When I told him I saw Mr. Davis looking at some sort of blueprint-type thing on his computer, so maybe he was an architect, and Gabriel frowned and said he thought that was very interesting, because why would an architect need to use an alias? It's very unsettling, Natalie."

Natalie chuckled. "Maybe he just wants privacy, and you two are very much encroaching upon that." Although, Natalie herself had been unsettled by Mr. Davis, so who was she to talk? "Oh! Maybe he's a celebrity. Or a movie director, and you were seeing a blueprint of a set design."

Natalie might have been jumpy yesterday, but she was working hard to calm her nerves. Helping Cora do the same was good for her. It kept her grounded in reality.

"I didn't even think of that," Cora said slowly. "That could make sense. A movie set in a ski lodge and he's here getting ideas. And he has a name we would recognize and doesn't want to answer a bunch of questions."

"Exactly."

"Excuse me." Both ladies turned to see Gabriel standing in the entryway. "I'm sorry to bother you. I don't suppose you have any more cookies?" He winced. "Turns out I think much better when I'm fully stocked with the best cookies in existence. Also… I kind of locked myself out of my room."

"Sure thing," Cora said, chuckling. "I'll get a plate together for you. Natalie can get you a new key, and I'll bring the cookies to your room in just a few minutes. I've got to take these up anyway." She grabbed an armload of fresh, folded towels, and left the room, humming.

"They're still talking about that guy, huh?" Gabriel said, nodding toward the TV.

"Ugh, yes, and Cora can't get enough of it, unfortunately," Natalie said. She picked up the last towel and began folding it, but then looked at the TV screen full-on for the first time.

And the entire world dropped out from under her.

She froze, unable to make her hands or her eyes move, barely able to make herself breathe.

On the TV screen was a mug shot of the fugitive prisoner. Hair unruly, wild look in his eyes, but otherwise, looking just like anybody's next door neighbor. One who might help you unlock your apartment door if your hands were full with groceries and your key wasn't working right. One you were developing a crush on and might be thinking would be interesting to date.

One who would attack you when you least expected it, rob you and leave you for dead at the bottom of a staircase.

Natalie blinked, hoping that maybe she was seeing things incorrectly. That any blond man in a mug shot might look familiar to her. But then the name of the fugitive flashed across the bottom of the screen, and just to be certain, the newscaster said it aloud.

Jed Grunder.

The runaway prisoner was Jed Grunder.

You're dead.

"Are you okay?" Natalie heard, distantly, behind her, as if Gabriel were asking from the other side of the county rather than the other side of the room.

She felt herself nod slowly, but her hands were still frozen, and she realized she was clutching the towel with a viselike grip. "I just… I know that man," she said.

"What man? The fugitive? Jed Grunder?"

She nodded again, opened her mouth to speak, but in that instant, everything came back to her. Not just the attack itself, but the months back and forth to the police station, the weeks in the courtroom. Watching as Jed Grunder's family stared at her with hatred in their eyes.

Jed Grunder's family.

Which included his brother, John.

"John Davis," she said. "That's where I've seen him before."

"What? I'm sorry, I'm not following. Do you need to sit down?"

She turned to Gabriel, her fingers suddenly loosening and letting the towel fall to the floor and puddle around her feet. "John Davis," she repeated. "I've seen him before. He's John Grunder. Jed's brother."

"You look pale," Gabriel said. "Can I get you a glass of water or something?"

"Lock the doors," Natalie said, terror creeping up her throat, making it feel squeezed shut. "Cora's right. We need to lock the doors." She didn't wait for Gabriel to move. She brushed by him and careened toward the front door, knocking the tray of cookies off of a table on her way. It crashed to the floor, breaking into pieces, but she barely even heard it. She twisted the lock, her throat feeling tight.

John Davis would come back, and he would, reasonably, expect to be let back in. His things were, presumably, still here. He was a paying customer. And, besides, the storm had gotten started. Ice ticked against the lodge windows; wind gales bent the treetops sideways. Soon it would be snowing, and with that wind, visibility would be zero. Could she really lock a man out of the lodge in those conditions?

She would call the police. That's what she would do. Call them and let them know that her attacker's brother was in her lodge at the very same time that her attacker had escaped prison, and surely that was no coincidence.

But, even if the police wanted to talk to John Davis, his staying in her lodge wasn't exactly an arrestable offense. And that was if the police could even make it up here in the bad weather.

Suddenly, Gabriel was by her side. No longer asking questions. No longer trying to get up to speed. Just following her lead as she headed through the kitchen and to the back door that, as Cora pointed out, they weren't always the best at keeping locked.

The door was standing wide open.

"We don't ever leave it like this," she said, mystified, even though on some level she knew exactly what this meant. She felt all the blood leave her head, and for a second, she felt swimmy. *Leave*, a voice inside of her said. *You've known for days that something was off, that someone was watching you. For once in your life, trust your gut. Just go. Don't even think about it. Get out.*

Gabriel stepped past her, through the door into the wind and snow outside, and looked around. He came back in. "Nobody," he said. "Maybe Cora...?"

Cora.

Natalie needed to alert Cora.

"She's upstairs delivering towels," she said, and in that exact moment, there was a noise from above.

A short shriek, followed by tumbling footsteps and a loud thump.

Gabriel's eyes met Natalie's, and without a word, they raced for the stairs.

"Cora!" Natalie shouted, panic in her voice.

Gabriel had no idea what was going on. But it didn't take a detective—private or otherwise—to see that something had rattled Natalie to the bone. She seemed certain that she knew the fugitive who was all over the news. And, if Gabriel was piecing things together correctly, she knew his brother, as well. And she seemed to think John Davis was that very man.

It also didn't take a detective to know that something had happened with Cora upstairs.

But when they reached the top of the stairs, they were met with a quiet hallway. All doors shut. Like any other lodge.

Natalie stopped in her tracks, her breath heaving. She licked her lips, her eyes darting from door to door.

"Should we call for her?" Gabriel whispered.

Natalie shook her head. "It sounded like she was down there," she whispered, pointing with one shaky finger at the rooms at the other end of the hall. She took one step forward, and Gabriel followed. Side by side, they rushed down the hall, every creak of floorboard sounding to Gabriel's ears like an announcement over a loudspeaker. *Here we come! Get ready for us!*

Part of Gabriel wanted to believe that they'd only thought they'd heard something. That they would bump into Cora coming out of one of the rooms, still humming, still carrying an armload of towels, and that they would feel silly for working themselves up to believe that they'd heard something else. Part of him wanted to believe that they would end this little walk down the hallway laughing over a plate of cookies downstairs. TV off, of course.

But they never ran into Cora.

As they got farther down the hall, Natalie's steps seemed to get lighter and slower, as if she knew she was approaching danger. He could tell by the way she held her head perfectly straight that she was listening for more signs of where Cora could be.

But it didn't take hard listening to know.

There were thumps and bumps coming from inside the room that Gabriel knew to be John Davis's. He was both surprised and not surprised. And when Natalie's round eyes locked with his again, he could see she felt the same dreaded certainty washing over her. He stopped walking and inclined his head slightly to indicate that he was ready to do whatever needed to be done.

Together, they crept to the door. Natalie gently pressed her hands against the wood and leaned her ear toward it. After a second of listening, she nodded a confirmation at Gabriel—someone was in there.

They had to get inside that room. That much was clear. It was just a matter of how. He lowered his shoulder and gave a quick jab to the air to indicate that he could try to bust his way in. Even in all of his work as an investigator, he'd never tried to break a door down, but he'd seen it enough times in the movies. He understood that it was a matter of where you hit the door, not necessarily how much force you hit it with. How hard could it be?

But Natalie shook her head. She reached into her pocket and pulled out a key card. Of course. A master key card.

Every fiber inside of Gabriel felt coiled and ready to spring. He buzzed with anticipation of what, or who, they might find on the other side of that door. He was ready to attack or defend, whatever Natalie and Cora needed the most.

Con, he thought. *You won't find this in law school, that's for sure… Or is that a pro?*

He gave Natalie a little nod to indicate he was ready. She nodded back and, with shaking hands, presented the key card to the door reader.

It seemed to happen in slow motion, but the light on the lock blinked twice and flashed green.

Natalie turned the handle and pushed the door in.

And then everything sped up. Gabriel barged into the room, keeping one arm wide to protect Natalie, who stepped in behind him. It took his brain a moment to process what he was seeing. A man—the man he'd seen on all the recent news reports—standing at the foot of the bed, his hands clenched into fists, his eyes boring into Natalie.

And Cora, unconscious and bleeding, at his feet.

He didn't know how Natalie knew this man, or what exactly was transpiring between them now. He only knew that Natalie was scared to death, that she'd been afraid this man had come to the lodge looking for her, and that he had hurt Cora.

Well, he knew one other thing. He knew that he couldn't let that happen.

Tensing his muscles, he took two steps toward the escaped prisoner. He never even saw John come out from behind the open door and close the distance between them fast.

"Gabriel! Watch out!" Natalie shouted.

Gabriel turned just in time to see John rear back and swing. He tried to duck and block, but he was too late. The room lit up bright white, and then everything went black.

Chapter Three

So it was true. Jed Grunder had escaped the penitentiary and headed straight for the lodge to exact the revenge he'd promised in the courthouse. The fact he even knew about the lodge told Natalie that he'd been spending at least some of his prison time plotting and planning. Making good on his vow to kill her.

And he clearly had enlisted help.

Natalie couldn't unsee it now. The man who she'd felt she knew but couldn't place was John Grunder, and, though he'd grown a beard and now wore glasses, how his face ever became unfamiliar to her, she would never understand. She thought every detail of the entire trial had been seared into her memory forever.

Now this image of Cora lying on the floor at Jed's feet would be seared into her memory, even though she had only seconds to take it in.

Cora. Poor Cora. Lying with one leg bent uncomfortably back on itself. Natalie couldn't be sure if her best friend was alive or dead, and she didn't know how she would find out with Jed standing right over her.

Her eyes felt riveted to Jed's, her entire body frozen with fear. She felt as unmovable as a boulder. Part of her was still lying on the landing at the bottom of the stairs in her old apartment, waiting for Jed to finish the job he'd started. She was sure that she'd seen all of this in a nightmare, playing out in exactly this way.

She saw John come out from behind the door before Gabriel did. She screamed Gabriel's name, but she was too late. John swung, and though Gabriel ducked, John's fist still connected. Now Gabriel was sprawled on the floor just feet away from Cora, leaving nothing but open space between Natalie and Jed. And that seemed to be all it took for things to swim back into real time.

"Long time no see," Jed said through his teeth, his fists clenching so hard his knuckles looked white. And then with the litheness of a cat, he stepped over Cora and lunged at Natalie.

Natalie acted on impulse alone, her thoughts simple directives: *Don't let him touch you. Get away. Go hide.*

She turned and ran out of the room, barreling down the hallway with a speed she didn't know she had, her brain fast-sorting through options. She could hear his heavy footsteps behind her. He wasn't as fast as she was, but he wasn't slow, either. She wouldn't have time to key into a room without him seeing her. And if he followed her into a room, or broke a door down to get to her, she would be trapped.

She sprinted up the second flight of stairs, two at a time, and reached the top floor before him, her eyes and mind desperately searching for an answer.

And she saw one.

The laundry room. It just happened to be one of the few rooms in the Hideaway that had a regular lock rather than a keycard lock. She'd left it unlocked when she brought out that last load of towels. She knew she had, because her hands were full and she told herself she would lock it whenever she found herself upstairs again.

With a quick glance behind her to make sure Jed hadn't yet rounded the corner, she slipped into the laundry room, slapped off the light, and shut and locked the door.

There was a window in the door, but it was small and high and certainly didn't allow a view of the entire room. She didn't think she had time to find a good hiding place without him seeing her if she looked through the window, so she simply pressed herself against the wall next to the door, trying to be very still. Trying to silence her heavy breathing. Trying to make the little fireworks flashes behind her eyelids go away.

She wondered if both Jed and John were after her, or if John had stayed behind to finish what he'd started with Gabriel and Cora. She couldn't stand the thought of it.

Please, God, let Gabriel wake up in time to de-

fend himself, she begged. *Let him wake up in time to defend Cora.* The idea of being alone with Jed and John in the lodge hunting her was terrifying, but the idea of her best friend or this new man she'd come to like so much being hurt or killed tugged on her heart, making it ache.

It felt like only milliseconds before Jed's heavy footsteps were pounding down the hall toward her. How could it have even been possible that he hadn't seen her go into the laundry room? It wasn't. That was all there was to it. She had trapped herself in an even smaller room with even fewer chances of getting away. She inched toward the fire extinguisher on the wall next to her. If nothing else, she could use that as a weapon.

When Jed's body hit the door with a bang and shudder, she jumped and slapped a hand over her mouth to keep herself from crying out. She squeezed her eyes shut tight—*keep calm, keep calm, keep calm*—and then forced them open again, bracing herself for the crack and thud of the doorjamb giving way and the door flying open under Jed's shoulder. Natalie inched her free hand around the neck of the fire extinguisher, ready to pull. She would hit him with everything she had. She would aim for his face.

But after a rattle of the handle, Jed's weight lifted from the door and his footsteps thumped away. He went down the hall, banging menacingly on every room door. Natalie let out a shaky breath, her entire body tingling with release. Her knees buckled, and she slid down the wall, her head hanging low, her hands reaching for the ground between her knees. Every part of her was being taken back to the day in her apartment stairwell. But she knew she couldn't go there. Going there would cloud her focus, and she needed to focus. She had to get to Cora…and to Gabriel. Or at least get help for them.

"Okay," she whispered, the same thing she'd whispered to herself as she half crawled, half dragged herself down her apartment stairs, leaving a trail behind her. Hearing her own voice comforted her. As long as she was talking, she knew she wasn't dying. "Okay, okay." She took a deep, steadying breath and stood, then turned her eyes upward. "A little help here?"

As brave as she was ever going to be, she slowly peeked through the window. If he was standing on the other side, there would be no hiding. He would see her, and he would come for her.

But he wasn't there. The hallway was clear. She could dart into the room across the hall and call the police. She could do it. She knew she could, as long as she committed. No hesitation. Just act.

She wrapped her hand slowly around the doorknob. Silently, silently, she turned the knob. And then she pulled the door open and stepped out.

Jed Grunder was standing against the wall right next to the door.

He growled and lunged at Natalie, his fingers brushing her shirt.

She screamed, her hand reaching for the key card in her pocket.

Except there was no key card there.

* * *

Gabriel's head felt fuzzy and heavy. His ears were doing this thing that was sort of a cross between a hum and a ring. The room seemed too bright. His limbs were warm, buzzing with adrenaline. And the reason he was lying on the floor with a fuzzy head and buzzing limbs was temporarily out of his mind's reach.

But he wasn't afraid.

He saw boots coming toward him, and remembered that he wasn't alone in this room. He turned his head and saw Cora lying next to him, arms sprawled. He thought he saw slight movement—the tiniest frown between her eyebrows, the fleetest flick of a finger—and felt awash with relief. She wasn't dead. He wasn't dead. At least there was that.

But Natalie…

It was the thought of something happening to Natalie that caused him to spring into action. The room swam as he pulled himself to standing and faced John, who was quickly approaching. Gabriel was sure he was swaying more than standing, but he had no time to think about that. He had no choice but to be upright and make this work. And make it work quickly.

Gabriel had been taught at a young age that any prayer can be answered. Even the most unlikely, simplest prayer like, *Please, God, let me land this one punch*, and he fully intended to pray it. He squeezed his hand into a fist and felt his mouth draw down into a snarl as he drilled into John's eyes with his own.

"You don't want to do this," he said.

"You don't know what I want to do," John replied. A smile spread across his face, evil and creepy. "I'm actually going to enjoy this quite a lot."

"I'm not going to make it easy on you."

"You sure you want to die here? Why would you fight for her? You don't even know her, do you?"

"Neither do you," Gabriel said.

John threw his head back and laughed. "Oh, but I do. I know exactly what she did to my brother. If it wasn't for her, he wouldn't be in prison. They had nothing on him."

"Coming after her won't get him out of prison," Gabriel said. "And it will get you in there with him."

"It's the satisfaction," John said, feinting toward Gabriel, making him tense and put his fists up in front of his face. "And we'll only be in prison if we get caught. And we won't get caught. By the time anyone realizes something happened up here, we will be long gone. The storm wasn't part of our plan, but it is going to be very helpful." He feinted again and then sprang into action, but Gabriel was ready for him. At just the right moment, Gabriel reared back, swung with all his might, and connected.

His hand lit up with pain that radiated up his arm like a lightning bolt, but he only felt it from a distance. If something was broken, he would deal with it later. He waited for John to fall. One punch and out, just like had happened to him a moment before.

But John was bigger. Much bigger. And he'd turned his head at the last second, so that Gabriel's punch landed just above his ear, the pain in Gabriel's hand from connecting with John's skull. John stumbled back two steps, caught himself against a wall and squared up again, his lips still drawn back into that terrible smirk.

Gabriel tensed his shoulders, ready, as something inside of him bloomed into existence for the very first time—a fierce need to protect. Cora was still alive; he was sure of it. And if he acted fast enough, maybe he could get help in time to keep it that way. But, more importantly, Natalie was out there, very much alive. He'd felt a spark, a oneness between them, something he was pretty sure if fanned, would burn brighter. Possibly much brighter.

It was that spark that caused him to calm himself, to settle back into his stance. *Come on,* he said in his head. *I'm ready for you.*

When John drove forward, Gabriel was able to absorb the momentum only budging a few inches. They locked into each other, each grunting with the effort to push the other off balance. Gabriel wasn't really sure what his strategy was, only that he knew he needed to keep John as close as possible. It was hard to throw a real punch when you couldn't get any distance.

Still, John was able to work free enough to drive his fist into Gabriel's side, and then up into his ribs, a couple of them protesting painfully. Gabriel responded with close blows of his own, shoving John against the wall and quick-jabbing him in the jaw, the ear, the neck. John took all of the blows as if he'd felt nothing.

John grabbed Gabriel's shoulders and let out a growl, somehow gathering enough force to shove back Gabriel several steps, all the way to the bed, which cut his legs out from under him. He toppled backward onto the bed and went with the momentum, scrambling, rolling, until he was on his feet on the other side.

Gabriel knew that now John had the upper hand. He was closer to the door. He was closer to Cora. He was bigger.

But Gabriel was motivated.

When John came around the foot of the bed, trapping Gabriel between the bed and the wall, Gabriel reached back and grabbed the alarm clock off the nightstand.

He yanked so hard, the cord snapped out of the back of the clock, and so quickly, John didn't appear to even see it happen.

But he saw the clock. Up close and personal, as Gabriel brought it down on him, right above his left eyebrow. John fell to the floor, landing only a couple of feet away from Cora.

For a long moment, Gabriel bent low at the waist and simply breathed. How could such a small movement—such a short fight—take so much out of him? It was the adrenaline. It had to be. His own jaw began to ache where John had punched him earlier. But the pain felt like a memory. He knew it was there, but it was ignorable.

He heard groans coming from the floor. Cora had

begun to move her head, her face scrunched up with pain, her eyes still closed.

"Hey, hey, hey," he said, rushing to her. "Don't do that. Don't… I don't know what's hurt on you. Can you…can you open your eyes? Cora? Do you hear me?" Cora's eyelids gave the slightest flutter, as if she wanted to open them but couldn't quite muster the effort. It was enough for Gabriel. She was alive and she could hear and understand him.

But she was barely there. And she was surrounded by all this blood that appeared to be coming from the back of her head. And her movement seemed to be making it worse. How long before she wouldn't be okay anymore? How long until she wouldn't respond to him? To anyone at all?

"We've got to get you some help," he said. "We just need to…" His eyes drifted to John Grunder, who lay on the floor not far away. "Okay. Yeah. Okay. Let's…"

He knew that you should never move an accident victim, just in case there was something wrong that movement could make worse. But he also knew elevating Cora's head could make the bleeding slow down some, and that seemed like the more pressing issue at the moment. Plus, he hated that she was on the floor, especially if he was going to have to leave her there.

He scooped her up, one arm under her knees and the other under her back, letting her head rest on his bicep, and moved her to the bed, taking care to rest her upper body on the mountain of pillows that she had probably fluffed herself earlier that morning.

"I'm sorry about the blood on the pillowcase," he said. "You can yell at me later. In fact, I want you to yell at me later. Yell loud, and throw your hands in the air and shake your head like I'm despicable, okay?"

Of course, she didn't respond. He didn't expect her to. But he needed to believe she heard him and was making plans to do exactly that, as soon as she got this annoying, little head wound taken care of.

He reached down and pulled a blanket off the end of the bed, placing it carefully over her. He didn't know if she was hot or cold or if it even mattered—he just wanted her to know that he cared. "I'll be back for you." He looked over his shoulder, as if he were looking out into the corridor, and corrected himself. "*We* will be back for you."

But first, he had to take care of the problem currently writhing itself awake on the floor nearby. Gabriel did what he did best—the thing that made him a great PI, actually. He quickly assessed the situation and the area, and let his gut guide his actions.

He couldn't keep fighting with John. The longer he did that, the higher the chance he would lose, leaving Cora and Natalie at John's mercy. Also the longer he fought with John, the longer he left Natalie to fend for herself against Jed, and that was unacceptable.

He had to subdue John.

Gabriel hurried around the bed and went to the window. Unlike in most hotels, the pull cord on the Hideaway's blinds wasn't a continuous loop chain, which would have been difficult, if not impossible, to break. These were regular blinds with regular cord pulls. He grabbed ahold of one and yanked, feeling it snap free from the blinds and go limp in his palm. Then he wasted no time rushing back around the bed and falling to his knees next to John, who'd begun to mumble and feebly paw at the floor as if he was going to push himself upright.

"I don't think so," Gabriel said. He grabbed one wrist and used his bodyweight to flip John to his stomach, then grabbed the other wrist and pulled it behind his back.

Alarmed by what was obviously about to happen, John's struggles grew more intense, and Gabriel had to use all of his weight to hold John's arms down while he wound the cord around his wrists and knotted it a half-dozen times. Blood from a gash on his own cheek—probably from John's ring—dripped down and seeped into the fabric of John's sleeve, and only then did Gabriel feel the tickle of the blood dripping. He shrugged one shoulder and wiped the blood onto his shirt.

With the cord knotted and John's wrists secured, Gabriel sat back on his heels and wiped the sweat from his brow, trying to catch his breath.

He heard another unsettled noise from Cora—it sounded like she was trying to say Natalie's name but couldn't quite remember how to pronounce it—and he looked over at her again. The amount of blood already on the pillowcase, a growing crown atop her head, was alarming. He had to get help to her before it was too late.

He stood, staring at John. The man was no mountain, but he was big enough. And Gabriel wasn't sure what would be worse—if John fought him, or if he was deadweight in his arms.

He turned John over and grabbed him under the arms, and the answer came to him quickly. John began thrashing in Gabriel's hands, kicking his legs and pushing back against Gabriel, trying to stand. Gabriel grunted and gasped as he pulled John. He was never going to get him out of this room if he kept thrashing like this. He had to think of something else to do.

He released John, letting him thump down to the floor. John immediately began wiggling, trying to get his knees beneath him, spouting threats the entire time.

As a general rule, Gabriel was not in favor of hitting a defenseless man. And with his hands bound behind his back like this, John was certainly defenseless. But there was too much on the line. Cora needed medical attention, and he needed to find Natalie before Jed could get to her, if he hadn't already.

Gabriel tilted his eyes toward the ceiling. "Forgive me for this," he said aloud, then wound back and brought his fist around. The punch landed. He watched as John's furious expression changed to one of surprise, and then he was down again, his head lolling back uselessly. Gabriel shook out his hand and grabbed the other pillow from the bed. He whipped off the pillowcase, rolled it and tied it around John's mouth, careful to make sure that he could still breathe. He didn't want the guy yelling for his brother, but he didn't want to kill the guy, either. Satisfied that John

was silenced, Gabriel scrambled to grab him under
his arms again. He was much easier to drag when he
wasn't thrashing. Gabriel pulled John across the room
and into the hallway, propping the heavy wooden door
against his hip while navigating the limp man over
the threshold of the doorway.

The door shut behind them, putting Cora at a safe
and locked distance from the two men. Gabriel leaned
against the wall, catching his breath, feeling much
better about Cora's safety, with John crumpled in a
tied-up heap at his feet.

"Thank you, God," he said between breaths. "Now
if you could just lead me to Natalie…"

His prayer was cut short by Natalie's scream.

Chapter Four

Jed was so close, she could've reached out and touched his face. In the flash of terror that ran through her, she saw every stubble-studded pore in his jaw, the red blood vessels in his eyes, the angry, black pupils that were huge in the dim hallway light. The corners of his mouth, turned down in a grimace of fury. He looked older—much older—than he had when she last saw him. Harder, too. Angrier, if that was even possible.

She felt a rush as if being launched back through time. She'd been looking right at his face then, too. Smiling at him. Relieved that he was going to help her get her ancient, flimsy key—stuck and bending in the lock of her front door—out without breaking. She'd been thinking she would invite him to come inside for a cup of tea as a thank-you, a natural next step in what she thought was their friendly, flirty relationship. If she played her cards right, she was confident that eventually this would lead to a first date. And maybe more.

Oh, thank goodness, it's you, she'd breathed. *I have all these groceries and I can't get into my...*

She hadn't even gotten the word *apartment* out before his face turned into the grim flat line of determined anger.

She'd actually looked away. Over her shoulder. She'd been so surprised by this switch of personality in Jed, she'd thought maybe he was seeing someone coming up the stairs on the other side of her. That maybe he was going to protect her from someone else. Ha.

But there was no one coming, and instead there was the yank of her purse being pulled away from her. She'd screamed and the groceries had tumbled. She'd made the mistake of trying to hold on to her purse, and she would forever wonder if that was why he felt the need to hurt her. If she'd just let go, maybe he would have disappeared back down the hallway. Maybe he would have run, afraid of being picked up by the police, and she would have never seen him again.

But Natalie wasn't a give-up-and-let-the-bad-guy-win kind of woman. She was a fighter. To her own detriment? Maybe. She couldn't change who she was. She was a fighter then, and she was a fighter now.

And she definitely wasn't going to let him catch her in her own lodge.

"Long time no see," Jed growled, reaching for her, and that voice—*Sure, let me help you with your bag first*—loosed something in Natalie. Her feet no longer felt frozen.

She bolted away, feeling the flutter of his fingers as he grabbed at the back of her shirt, the sharp tightening of the fabric being caught, followed by an abrupt loosening as she moved too quickly and with too much power for him to hold on. He gave a short growl, and she could feel more than hear his heavy footsteps on the floor behind her.

She had to be quicker than him. Had to be. There was no choice. If she slowed at all, she knew what awaited her. She knew he wouldn't stop at a few broken bones and a concussion at the bottom of a flight of stairs this time. He would finish the job he'd started seven years ago. It had been his promise.

She needed to get into a room. Lock the door between them. Preferably the same room where Cora and Gabriel were.

Cora and Gabriel. Were they even alive? Natalie's gut twisted at the very thought. She couldn't let herself go down that path. They were alive. They had to be.

She couldn't be on this mountain with Jed Grunder and his murderous brother all alone.

Natalie ran back down the stairs, her feet pounding hard on the floor, and reached into her pocket again, searching for the key card. It wasn't there. She checked her other pocket. Not there, either. She remembered having it in her hand when they busted into the room where Cora had been. But she didn't remember anything about it after that. She had dropped it. Had to have. But where? In that room? In the laundry room? At some point in between?

In the end, it didn't really matter. She was without a key, so she couldn't very well put a barrier between her and Jed, now, could she? She reached the second floor, flew left, continued down the hall to the back staircase, and listened. There were footsteps behind her; that was for sure. But it almost seemed like more than one pair.

Please...be Gabriel, she thought.

And, as if in answer to a prayer, she heard Gabriel's voice.

"Natalie? Natalie! Where are you?"

He'd gotten away. She wasn't sure what that meant for Cora and for John Grunder, but Gabriel was alive, he was looking for her and that was enough.

"Gabriel!" she shouted, surprised by the volume of her own voice. "I'm..."

But she didn't get to finish. Jed had popped around the corner behind her. He was slowing down, breathing hard. She could outrun him if she had the space to pull away.

But not in these hallways. It was too easy to be found.

She knew what she had to do—lose Jed Grunder. She had to get to the place where she felt most comfortable.

She had to get outside. Onto the mountain.

Without a second thought, and only hearing Gabriel from a distance, she plunged down the stairs to the ground floor, her shoes slipping on the shiny wood as she barreled toward the front door.

She whipped open the door, and the storm slapped

her in the face with a gust of wet wind. She grimaced against the cold, but it didn't deter her in the least. She was far more afraid of Jed than she was of Mother Nature.

Natalie started to close the door and then remembered Gabriel. If she left the door open, hopefully he would follow. If he got outside, he would know where she went. Just to be safe, she called out to him. "I'm overthinking!"

She plunged out into the blizzard, disappearing from view almost instantly, only the faint impressions of her footsteps letting anyone know that she'd gone.

Natalie was alive. Thank God she was alive.

And from the sounds of the footsteps, she was up and running.

Unfortunately, from the sound of things, so was Jed Grunder. Running after her. Chasing her down.

"Gabriel! I'm..." She hadn't finished her sentence. She'd probably realized that if she told Gabriel where she was, she was likely telling Jed, as well. "I'm overth..."

The word was cut short, almost sounding whisked away by wind, but he knew what she was going to say. She was overthinking. It was a clue. His connection with Natalie on the ledge had been so instant, he knew exactly where she was going.

Gabriel tried to keep his steps light as he trod down the hallway. If he could slip out without Jed seeing him, he could connect with Natalie, and they could decide what to do next. He was impressed with Natalie's grit and relieved they were able to divide and conquer to get away from John and Jed, but he knew they would be stronger together. He'd just be able to think more clearly if he was sure Natalie was okay.

He slipped from shallow doorway to shallow doorway, trying to see without being seen. These were the skills that made him such a good fit for private investigation.

Too good of a fit, he told himself many times over. If it hadn't been for his PI skills, he might have never known that Liane was seeing his best friend on the side. The man he'd planned to ask to be his best man. Gabriel wasn't sure which was the bigger wound; he only knew he'd never put himself in that vulnerable position again.

But he was pretty vulnerable here, wasn't he? He wouldn't be the man he wanted to be if he left Natalie and Cora alone to contend with Jed and John.

The wind, howling against the lodge, gusted mightily. The lights flickered overhead, giving the hallway an even eerier atmosphere. Jed had probably followed Natalie, but he could just as easily have stayed behind and was waiting at the front door for Gabriel to happen by.

The back door. Of course. There was the back door. He and Natalie had been standing in it when they heard Cora get attacked. They'd come up a back staircase that led right to the hallway Gabriel was now standing in. Now that he thought about it, that was probably exactly how Jed had gotten into the Hideaway. John had sneaked him in through the back door and up the stairs.

Gabriel reversed direction and slipped back the way he'd come, past his own room and to the dead-end hallway that housed two lonely rooms, a utility room and a fire door. Staircase.

He paused at the doorway. Jed knew about this staircase. What if he was behind the fire door right now, waiting for Gabriel to pop through, correctly guessing that Gabriel would want to avoid the front door? A kitchen was at the bottom of this staircase. A kitchen full of knives.

He would have to rely on the element of surprise.

He tensed every muscle in his body as he placed the flat of his hand against the door. He wrapped his other hand around the doorknob and took a deep breath. Mentally counting to three, he simultaneously turned the knob and shoved the door. It opened easier than he thought it would, and it smashed into the wall with a booming thud that reverberated through the silent building and made Gabriel wince and hold his breath. He'd been so determined to knock out a waiting Jed with a smack of the door that he hadn't even thought about what would happen if Jed wasn't there.

But he probably would be very soon.

Sloppy. Gabriel was better than this. He specialized in being a silent presence slithering in and out of spaces unheard. And here he'd just broadcast his whereabouts to everyone in the building.

No time to think about things. Gabriel scurried down the stairs, his feet quiet, until he got to the bottom, then raced through the kitchen and out the back door.

He bent an arm in front of his face so he could see enough to get his bearings, then disappeared around the side of the lodge, leaning forward against the driving wind. The snow was already ankle-deep in some spots, and the ice beneath had made it slippery. He was wearing tennis shoes, not boots, and jeans that quickly got clotted and dragged down with clumps of icy snow. The cold gripped him instantly.

Still, he had to keep going. There was no choice.

He plodded around to the front of the lodge and crouched behind the porch rail, surveying the area. He crept forward, careful not to slip, careful not to let the snow crunch under his shoes, careful not to breathe over the sighing of the wind.

There was nobody. No Jed. No Natalie.

But there were footprints. They led away from the front door, which Gabriel could now see was left slightly open. The footsteps left trails in the snow, as if their owner had been running, and they led right into the woods. Natalie. She'd done exactly what Gabriel had thought she would do. She wanted him to follow.

Her footsteps were quickly filling with new-fallen snow. But behind each one was another, fresher footprint.

Much larger.

Different tread.

Longer stride.

Gabriel stopped in his tracks. Jed had followed

Natalie outside. He was following her footsteps. She was going to lead him right to a ledge. A ledge that would be fatal if she fell. Or if she was pushed over.

Gabriel quickened his own steps to a trot, then a run. "Natalie!" he yelled. "Natalie!"

Chapter Five

Natalie knew that she wasn't alone out here. She'd heard Jed's breathing behind her from pretty much the moment she stepped out into the storm. *Don't look back*, she repeated to herself. *Don't look back. Don't look back.*

But it was impossible not to look back. Even if what she saw was increasingly more terrifying. The man whose energy had been flagging running through the hotel seemed to have gained speed and force on the mountain. Like a locomotive, steadily chugging toward her.

Natalie dug into the snow with her heels, creating cups of traction to propel herself forward and up, her leg muscles burning with each step. She'd learned this when trying to scale the mountain to fix problems with the lift, pick up trash dropped from the lift, any number of tasks. She was no longer worried about leaving tracks in the snow for Jed to follow; he could see her from the distance he was at anyway. Her best

bet now was to use the mountain to her advantage.
She knew the landscape. She was comfortable on it.
She could handle the cold. She could buy time until
Gabriel got out here.

Jed got to the Hideaway somehow, the doubtful
corner of her mind tried to argue. *He didn't drive.
He knows the mountain, too. He's been living on it
for days.*

She was only guessing that to be true. After all,
John had kept Cora out of his room from the beginning of his stay. For all they knew, John had driven
up to the Hideaway with Jed stowed away in his car,
and had been keeping him in his room this whole
time. Just biding time. Waiting.

When all the customers fled before the storm, leaving the lodge nearly empty, it had probably provided
him with exactly the scenario he was waiting for.

But she remembered the prints in the woods.
They'd looped toward the edge over and over again.
As if someone had been watching the lodge from
the cover of the trees. If he'd been living outside, he
might actually know the area better than she did. He
might know places that she'd never been.

Natalie glanced behind her. Jed was closer than
ever. She could see the puffs of his breathing, could
hear the grunts of his trying to stay upright. She
pushed uphill, hoping that she would eventually get to
a slope she could handle and he couldn't. She glanced
again, just in time to see him slip and fall, momentum
taking him down the mountain several feet before he
was able to stop himself.

She felt a moment of triumph, quickly followed by a drag of snow that tripped her up. She threw her weight forward and fell onto one knee, clawing into the snow with her hands to keep herself from sliding right into his reach, panic creating little stars in front of her eyes.

She stopped short and was up and dashing again. Her hands were numb now, as was her nose and her ears. She'd seen what frostbite did to people and had always been very vigilant about protection from the wind and snow. But she didn't have time to think about that now. She would have to fix whatever happened when this was all over.

Assuming I'm still alive when this is all over, she thought.

She chanced another glance. Jed was back on his feet but had fallen farther behind now. He was limping—probably jammed an ankle while trying to stop his momentum. The thought buoyed Natalie, and she turned up the gas on her own speed. When she glanced again, he was back on the ground, pounding the snow with his fists.

Natalie veered off of the slope and into the woods. Overthinking. She had told Gabriel she would be overthinking. She felt in her soul that he knew what she'd meant when she said that. Their connection on the ledge was so instant and so deep, it had scared her away at the time. But now she knew he would find her there, and they would face Jed together. They would figure out what to do.

Gravity and impatience teamed together to hasten her speed as she doubled back and raced down the mountain. She used trees for support, ricocheting from one to the next, her palms slapping the rough trunks, leaving little scrapes and stabs of splinters in her hands as she went. Faster and faster, deeper into the woods, racing for help. Guidance. Escape.

She was so focused on what would be waiting for her once she got there, she forgot to pay attention to where she was. She chanced the tiniest glance over her shoulder—Jed was just a speck on the outside edge of the woods now—and when she looked forward again, it was too late to veer around the birch that had come right to her.

She got her hand up just in time to shield her face from the worst of the blow but still felt the impact reverberate through her entire body. Her forehead struck the wood and down she went, tumbling, tumbling, her body bouncing from trunk to trunk the way her hands had been doing only moments before.

When she finally skidded to a stop, the world spun around her. She blinked as snowflakes landed in her eyes. They were beautiful. An undulating curtain of white lace against a wooded backdrop. The wind, too, was lovely, a sigh and a song combining into a symphony that cradled her, puffed against her numb limbs, kept them from feeling the pain of having taken the fall.

With the numbness, she had no way of knowing if anything was broken. She felt a warmth trickle down the side of her face and pool with a tickle in her ear. She reached up, and her hand came away wet with blood. The tree had split a line of skin across her forehead.

I could die here, she thought. *But at least this is way more beautiful than the bottom of a filthy staircase in an apartment stairwell.* And with that thought, she jolted, remembering where she was, why she was running in the first place.

"Gabriel," she said aloud, and began the monumental task of getting herself upright, blinking the snow out of her eyes, while everything swam in her vision. "I can't… I can't…"

She had managed to flip over to her hands and knees—so far everything felt intact—and was staring at the dots of blood that dripped onto the snow, trying to clear her mind, thinking that she needed to be moving with much more urgency, when she felt a pair of arms wrap around her from behind and lift her to her feet.

Natalie fought. She screamed and kicked and flailed her arms and bucked her entire body, making herself nearly impossible to hold on to.

"It's me," Gabriel said, clamping a hand on her waist to keep her from falling out of his grasp. "Natalie, stop. It's me. It's Gabriel."

It took another few seconds for her to seem to register who had ahold of her. She slowed rather than stopped entirely, gasping the entire time, nearly knocking both of them to the ground.

"It's me," he said quietly, when she had finally stopped fighting. He set her feet on the ground and let go. Once he was sure that she could stand alone, he took a couple of steps backward, alarmed by how much relief he had felt at getting to hold her in his arms.

She spun and confronted him. Her face went from alarm and fear to joyous recognition. "Oh, Gabriel," she said. "It's you." She wrapped him in a hug so exuberant, he had to use one hand to stabilize them against a tree. "I thought you were him," she said into his shoulder. "I was worried you were still…"

"In the lodge," he finished for her. "No. And neither is Jed. He's following you."

She released him and stepped back, peering over his shoulder. He resisted the urge to wipe the blood from her forehead. It seemed to have stopped gushing and was more seeping into drying rivulets now, strands of her hair stuck in place. He could feel himself shivering, and knew that he should feel cold, out in a blizzard without even so much as a light jacket, but the adrenaline of finding Natalie alive and okay was keeping him warm.

"I know," she said. "I was running from him. I was trying to get to…"

"The ledge. I was coming to meet you there, too," he finished. They both watched as Jed, who had apparently fallen again, lay panting in the snow, his arms flayed out wide.

"Come on, there's a couple of bushes over here we can hide behind while he's not looking." Natalie's thinking seemed clearer now. She grabbed Gabriel's hand and pulled him along, expertly stepping between roots that were barely hidden by the snow. "Watch your footing here." She crouched and ducked and pulled him through the thicket.

The ledge bloomed before them on the other side, the sight so majestic, it nearly took Gabriel's breath away. Trees wearing snow caps like hats and the bluish-black ice of the pond being covered over with flakes. A rabbit hopped lazily around the bottom of a tree, stopping to chew on a found treasure. A small cloud floated beneath them, giving the illusion that they could step right off of this ledge and walk on it, lie down for a nap. And to think if they hadn't been out here running from Jed, he would have never seen this view.

"Up here," Natalie said, dropping his hand as she used her fingers to claw her way up into a little grove. She stayed crouched, peering through the evergreen leaves, watching for Jed. Gabriel could barely tear his eyes away from the view, but when he looked, he didn't see anything anyway.

"Maybe he gave up," he whispered.

"Maybe," she said, but she didn't sound convinced. She gingerly prodded at the wound on her forehead and hissed. "Is it bad?" she asked.

"It could use stitches, but I think you'll be okay. I saw you fall," Gabriel said. "I tried to stop you, but you were falling too fast."

Worry creased her face. "What about John?"

"He's taken care of. I got him out of Cora's room."

"Is he out here, too?"

Gabriel shook his head. "He's tied up inside. He won't be going anywhere."

"What about Cora?" she asked, the pain in her eyes something different, something deeper.

He nodded. "Still alive and safe. But she's bleeding pretty badly. She needs help. We've got to get her help."

"It's this storm," Natalie said. "Nobody is going to be able to make it up here. Not easily, anyway."

"So we'll have to get her down."

Natalie chewed on her bottom lip pensively. "If I can get back into the lodge, I can grab my keys, and we can take my Jeep down. We've got to do what we can for her, Gabriel. It's not her that they want. It's me. She was just in the wrong place at the wrong time. You, too."

Gabriel couldn't take it anymore. He had to know what was going on. Maybe if he heard the whole story, he would come up with an idea that would help rescue them. "Why are they after you?"

Natalie couldn't seem to take her eyes off of the thicket, couldn't stop looking for Jed. It was almost as if she'd spent a lifetime looking over her shoulder for him.

"He attacked me. Years ago. We lived in the same apartment building. We were friends, or at least I thought we were." She shook her head. "Actually, I thought we were going to be more than friends. I was hoping he would ask me out on a date. He seemed… flirty."

"So obviously something happened between you."

"Yes. But not in that way. The apartment building was old and kind of falling apart, and the landlord wasn't doing a whole lot about it. The lock on my front door would stick sometimes. And the key was fragile, and it would bend when I tried to turn it. I thought it was going to break off in the lock.

"I had just gone to the grocery store and had all these bags. I'd bought a lot of stuff. I was going to throw a birthday party for my friend that night. I was going to invite Jed to the party." She said this with a look of bewilderment, as if it was a detail that she was just now remembering, or maybe she hadn't considered the full ramifications of before. She swallowed, shook it off. "My lock was stuck, as usual, and my key was bending, and I was juggling all these bags, and here he came from out of nowhere. I was actually relieved."

She shook her head again and stared down at the snow. Gabriel wanted to reach out and soothe her, but now didn't seem like the right time. He sensed she needed him to listen more than anything else.

"I thought he was going to help me, but he…he robbed me instead. Took my purse. Beat me up and shoved me down the stairs. Went inside and took whatever he could get his hands on."

"He hit you?" Gabriel felt himself flush with anger. Jed had hurt her and was now back to hurt her again.

"He more than hit me. He beat me pretty severely. He kicked me—literally kicked my head and my ribs and my back—on his escape down the stairs. I'm pretty sure he thought I was dead. I almost was. He was trying to kill me."

Gabriel wasn't prepared for the well of rage that rose in him. Natalie was delicate and kind and friendly and deep. How could someone treat her so cruelly? "I'm sorry," he said, his voice gruff with so many things that he wanted—and did not, would not—say.

"I woke up in the hospital about three weeks later. At first, I had no idea what happened. It was all—" she waved her palm around her head "—blank. A void."

"I'm sure that was really frightening," Gabriel said.

"It was terrifying." She shuddered. "But I started remembering things. Flashes. The boot coming at my head especially. And I remembered who did it to me. So I turned him in. And then I worked with the prosecutor to make sure they threw everything they had at him. I found three other girls who said he did this to them, too, but they were afraid to go to police when they thought it was only them. They were scared. I was scared."

"Of course you were," Gabriel said. "Anyone would be."

"But more than scared, I was determined. I wanted him to be put away forever for what he did. He got thirty years for attempted murder. I was there for the entire trial. I wanted his family to see me. To see what happened to me. To hear it from my own voice. The only family that showed up for him was his brother. John. I'd forgotten about him until today."

"But we would never forget about you." The voice came from above.

Gabriel looked up just in time to see Jed standing over them, about four feet away, on the other side of the shrub. He looked winded. Spent. Cold. Tufts of his hair stuck out in wild directions. His shirt was ripped. He was bleeding from one bicep.

And he looked happy.

Giddy, even. Unhinged.

"We've been thinking about you this whole time," Jed said, taking a step closer. "We just can't rest until we know that you're…resting." Another step.

"Run, Natalie!"

But Natalie seemed fused to the spot. Her jaw was set, and Gabriel could sense anticipation in her. She wasn't paralyzed by fear; she was refusing to budge out of principle.

Gabriel was going to have to act now. He stepped out from behind the bush and tackled Jed, burying his shoulder in Jed's side, reminiscent of his days playing high school football. They hit the ground with an *oof*, and Gabriel quickly lost Natalie in the chaos that ensued. Jed Grunder was not going to go down easily. He was stronger than his brother. Wirier and quicker, too. And he fought with a ferocity of someone who had spent a good deal of time in desperation. His fists landed like hammers against Gabriel's skin, but Gabriel refused to give up. He held on to Jed's shirt, kept him in close where he couldn't get much momentum with his swing.

"Natalie! Go!" he yelled, having no idea whether

or not she was still standing there. But then he heard her voice, steady, loud.

"I'm the one you want," she said. "Leave him alone and come after me."

He thought he heard a slight waver under the word *me*. She was bluffing. And she was doing it to save Gabriel.

With a roar, Jed shoved against Gabriel, almost breaking his grip. Gabriel kept his fists clenched with everything he had, biding time. *Just let her get away,* he thought. *Do whatever you need to do with me, but let her go.*

The trees shuddered as a gale of wind forced its way through, showering them with snow that had been caught in the leaves. Gabriel began to wonder how long before someone would freeze to death out here, and he was pressed with an absurd mental image of the two of them being locked in a frozen grip, a deadly ice sculpture. There was something about the solitude of it all that reminded him that they were truly alone up here. Literally everyone had gone. And help was a long way away, if they could reach it at all. If Natalie didn't get to the Jeep soon, they may not be able to traverse the mountain to find help anyway. And how long could the two of them fend off these desperate men?

He didn't hear Natalie run away. He was solely focused on his wrestling match with Jed, whose thrashing seemed to get uglier, but maybe a bit weaker. Perhaps Gabriel could wear him down. He clenched his hands tighter around the fabric.

When Jed finally pulled from Gabriel's grip, his shirt snapping through Gabriel's numb fingers while Gabriel's hands still remained in fists, he shoved Gabriel away. Gabriel stumbled backward, his heel meeting a jutting rock. Down he went, gravity taking him head over heels all the way to the ledge.

He tumbled over.

Chapter Six

Natalie certainly wasn't going to run to the lodge.
Gabriel was holding Jed, but she knew he couldn't
hold him forever, and if she trapped herself inside
the lodge with Jed, she would be right back where
she started. Running down empty hallways, getting
nowhere, trying to avoid him until she just couldn't
any longer. They were rats in a maze, and she was
pretty sure that she was the cheese.

Plus, she couldn't just leave Gabriel. Not after he
so bravely took on Jed to give her time to run away.
She had to make sure he was okay.

Her plan wasn't a bad one. Get the Jeep key. Get
down the mountain. The only problem was Cora.

Could she just leave Cora?

She didn't think she could. Her master key was
missing—likely dropped in the room where Cora
was—but there was a spare. She would have to re-
trieve the other master key and somehow get Cora
into the Jeep. She knew she couldn't do that alone.

She needed Gabriel. Gabriel wasn't about to let go of Jed until he was either overpowered or certain that she'd gotten away.

Hiding spot. She needed a good hiding spot until she could figure out exactly what to do.

Hiding spot. Of course.

Natalie raced toward the lodge, taking care to step in the spots under the eaves where the snow was sparse. She made her way around back, startling Felix, who spiraled up his tree, and made a beeline for the spruce tree where she'd seen the deer the day before. She prayed that the deer had only been snacking, and she wouldn't find herself eye-to-eye with a protective mama deer in a den.

She parted the branches and crawled under the tree. No defensive mamas or hungry babies, just a warm little respite from the wind and snow, a soft carpet of evergreen beneath her.

She suddenly felt so tired. So drained. Almost pulsating with weariness, as if she could simply curl up on the ground and fall asleep. Forget about John and Jed Grunder. Forget about Cora's attack. Forget that any of this had ever happened, starting all the way back in her apartment hallway.

She was surprised that she opened up to Gabriel about the attack. It was something she didn't talk about. Not even Cora knew. It was too painful. Too real. But somehow she just knew that Gabriel was the right person to open up to. He'd seemed so deeply engrossed in the story. She could almost feel him wishing he'd been there to protect her.

At times she wondered what had given her the strength to pull through after that attack. And in that moment behind the shrubs when she had told Gabriel the tale, she'd been so drawn into the moment with him, it almost seemed like she survived for him. Even though they didn't know each other at the time.

It was a surreal feeling, like they were brought together for a reason. But not just now. Like they were already together in spirit before they even met.

Oof, she must have hit her head harder than she thought. She pressed her fingers into the wound, which had dried. Or frozen. It was kind of hard to tell.

Now that she was someplace warm, the shivering started. And the pins and needles, which lit up her fingers and toes and even the tips of her ears. Her nose ran and her eyes watered, and she knew that Gabriel was still out there in the storm, which only made her feel colder. They were fighting more than just this fugitive and his brother; they were fighting the elements, too.

She closed her eyes. *God, if You could just... I don't know...give Gabriel a boost? A little extra strength? Do You do that? Can I just order up extra strength like I'm choosing a brand of deodorant? That's crazy. Maybe I should concentrate on thinking rational thoughts. Okay, God? Are You there? Are You even listening? If You are, get Jed away from Gabriel. Help us save Cora.*

Natalie wasn't sure how she felt about God. After the attack, she'd all but written Him off. How could a loving God allow something so awful to happen to such a faithful servant? But in this moment, she found herself calling on God to protect Gabriel. To draw Jed away from him. To keep Cora alive.

She had no expectations that God would hear her prayer, and even fewer expectations that He would answer it, but only moments later, she heard the huff and cough of labored breathing, at first riding on top of the wind, and then coming closer. She pressed her face into the pine needles and peered out, being careful not to let herself be seen from the outside.

Please be Gabriel, please be Gabriel...

But instead it was Jed, making his way across the lift area and back toward the lodge. He seemed singularly focused on getting inside. Natalie pulled back and bit her lip to keep her own breathing from being heard. She stayed as still as the little deer who'd surprised her under this tree.

Jed lumbered up the porch and into the lodge. Natalie peered into the woods, watching and waiting for Gabriel. But when she didn't see him, she counted to ten and made her move. Something was very wrong. Gabriel wouldn't have easily let Jed get away, and even if he'd allowed him out of his grasp, he would have followed him.

Unless he couldn't.

The thought made Natalie feel so numb, her legs didn't want to work. She slogged through, each step feeling like it carried a thousand-pound weight, as if she were in waist-high snow, or mud, or quicksand, the woods getting deeper and deeper, as if it were growing away from her, expanding the distance between her and Gabriel.

When she came upon the cleared spot in the snow, where their shoes had kicked and pressed all the way through to the ground, she wasn't sure if she was relieved or terrified to see that Gabriel wasn't there. Only Jed had gone back to the lodge—she was sure of it—so where had Gabriel gone?

She was almost afraid to look around, scared that she would find him looking like Cora—lifeless and bleeding. And then she would truly be on her own and would be trying to figure out how to get him out of the storm so he didn't freeze to death.

But then she heard what sounded like something scraping against rock. She wheeled, half expecting to see Jed having doubled back and standing right behind her, ready to finish her off, and half expecting to see a bear, the scraping sound a claw ready to let loose on her.

But she saw nothing. No one. And the origin of the sound seemed to have shifted. She wheeled again, and again. Maybe she was going crazy.

Maybe it was Gabriel.

She was going to have to call out for him. Which could draw Jed back to her. But she had to take the chance. Gabriel was out here somewhere, and she needed to be with him.

"Gabriel?" she called softly, and then a little louder. "Gabriel? Is that you?"

She heard a grunt and more shuffling. Someone was definitely out here with her. But it sounded like it was coming from the ledge itself. Surely...

She didn't know how she possibly missed it before. The circle of mussed snow was much bigger than she thought, and it led dangerously close to the ledge where she and Gabriel first met. It wasn't the same exact place—a few feet higher—but the men had definitely scuffled their way to the ledge. And, from the looks of things, one of them had gone over.

She gasped, pushing her fist to her mouth, her stomach dropping.

"No," she whispered. "No, no, no." If Gabriel had gone over the ledge, he was most certainly dead.

But as if in response to her fears, she heard the scuffle again, another grunt and a soft "Natalie?"

She wanted to scramble to him—to dive over the edge and get to him as quickly as possible. But she knew that would be deadly for her. Somehow, unbelievably, it hadn't been fatal for him.

She picked her way carefully over the slippery rock, toeing her way to the edge as if she'd never been there before. Better safe than sorry.

But also, she was delaying seeing what had happened to Gabriel.

When she finally got to the edge, she sank to her knees and carefully leaned over the edge. And sucked in a breath.

Gabriel was hanging on for dear life, his toes barely finding purchase on a tiny jutting rock.

If it gave way, he would fall to his death.

* * *

Gabriel had God to thank for a lot of things in life, but this one was probably the biggest thank-you owed by anyone ever. As soon as he'd started falling, his instincts had kicked in. He'd flipped himself to his stomach and dug his fingers into the earth as hard as he could. He knew he was still going to go over; he just wasn't going to go over easily.

When his fingers landed on a root that gave way just a tiny bit, he slammed into the rock face with his whole body, and somehow there was the tiniest foothold rushing up to meet the toes of his right foot.

It was all he had. But it was something.

He spent a long moment just breathing, letting his heart, which was certainly at the bottom of the canyon by now, rejoin the rest of his body. He pressed his cheek into the rock. It was like pressing against a block of ice, but it still felt beautiful. As his breath slowed, he'd matched it with praise. *Thank you, God. Thank you, God. Thank you.*

He had to start thinking about how he was going to get back up over that ledge.

And then he heard Natalie's voice. At first, he was convinced he was imagining it. Hearing what he wanted to hear. Natalie's voice meant Natalie was safe, and also that he now had help. If it was real...

When her face popped over the ledge, he nearly cried out yet another thank-you. She was real, and she was there.

And she was terrified.

"What happened?" she asked breathlessly, and

then, looked around wildly. "Okay. Okay, okay. We can... How are you even...? Just hold on."

"I plan to," Gabriel said. "But I can't feel my fingers or my toes anymore, so if I let go, you might be the first to know."

Her eyes grew wide. "Do not let go. Do not. Here. Grab my hand."

Gabriel shook his head forcefully. "Absolutely not. If I slip, we both die."

"You won't slip. I won't let you," she said. "As long as we work together, you'll be okay."

She was right. They would be stronger together. She was full of grit and determination, and he trusted that she would give this everything she had. He was sure that was how she'd survived Jed's attack the first time.

Gabriel momentarily lost footing on his left side. He cried out.

Natalie also cried out, but it was a cry of frustration more than anything. He dug in harder with his fingers, his legs scrambling until he was back in reach of the foothold he'd found. He was no rock climber, and his calves were on fire, but the footholds seemed to be his only chance of surviving.

"Are there more footholds?" he asked. "Can you see? I can't... I can't see anything."

"Are there what?" she said, but she was already leaning over the ledge looking. She shook her head. "No. Not up."

His heart panged. "Down? There are footholds down? How far down?"

"No," she said. "There aren't… Wait. Yes. Yes, I see some." She leaned so far over the edge, he feared she might plummet past him. Her fingers were red from the cold, and her entire body was shivering. "Not down. That way." She pointed at the rock face on his right, which was technically uphill.

The root that Gabriel was holding onto started to slide against his palms. He gripped with all of his might, resteadying himself. "Where? Lead me."

"Okay," Natalie said. She licked her lips and glanced behind her, presumably checking for the return of Jed, then squeezed her eyes closed and opened them again, her focus clear. "Two feet to your right and about six inches up. A little farther…a little…yes. You've got it. Now move your left foot to the hold your right foot was just on. Keep going. There. Now, do it again. This one's at about your hip level. You're going to have to step up onto it. Yes, yes, good."

The root gave slack as he stood on the foothold, and he felt his balance slide backward to where he nearly wheeled his arms, but caught himself at the last minute. He shifted his weight forward instead, pressing his body hard against the rock.

"Handhold," she said. "There's a handhold. Do you see it? It's right—yes, right there. Grab it. It'll be sturdier than the root you're holding onto. Okay, okay, you— No, not— Yes, there."

The wind pushed against him as he crept along the wall, inch by inch, Natalie as his eyes. He concentrated on her voice—calm, reassuring—and told himself that if he let go and fell to his death, the last thing he would have seen in this world would have been her. Delicate features, skin wind-chapped and rosy so that the freckles that rode the bridge of her nose actually stood out rather than being blotted away. Surrounded by all of this amazing nature, she was the natural beauty that most filled him with wonder.

When he found the foothold that would propel him up over the ledge, she grabbed his upper arms and pulled, and for the longest moment, they stayed in a hug, all of the what-ifs and might-have-beens clouding the air around them on the steam of their breath.

"Thank you," he breathed into her hair. "Thank you."

Chapter Seven

The decision was made quickly. If they were going to survive this, they had to get back inside. And if Cora was going to survive at all, they had to get help.

"Your keys," Gabriel said, bent over so that his forearms were resting against his thighs. Natalie could only imagine how spent his muscles must have felt. She felt rubbery herself, and she didn't do half the work that he did. His fingertips were scraped raw. "To the Jeep. Where are they?"

"They're in the lodge office," she said. "Along with my extra master key and my cell phone."

"Where is the office?"

"Right behind the front desk. All we need to do is get in the front door, and then slip in and slip right back out. The only thing…" She trailed off, staring into the distance, a worried look on her face.

"What?" he asked. "The only thing, what?"

"It's just that once we're in the office, we're trapped. There are no other doors, no windows. If

Jed were to come in behind us, the only way out is past him."

Gabriel stood, blew into his hands, alternately flexed them wide and balled them into fists, shook them out. "So I'll keep him from getting into the office," he said. "You go in, and I'll stand guard by the front desk."

Natalie wasn't so sure about this idea. Jed was stronger than Gabriel, and while before the ledge incident Natalie would have thought Gabriel would've been less tired than Jed, at this point she could see how taxed Gabriel was. She was afraid he would be easily overpowered by Jed.

Still, there was a fire in his eyes that told her he was ready to fight again. To protect her, if that was what she needed. She believed in him.

Her trust in him was certainly unexpected. She didn't think she would ever trust anyone—especially a man—again, yet here she was, nodding along to his plan of keeping watch for a killer while she rooted through her office for keys.

He was brave and cunning, yet at the same time, he didn't seem in the least bit bothered that she had saved him on the ledge. Quite the contrary. He seemed grateful. And as their embrace lingered, she couldn't help noticing that their hearts—both beating frantically—were somehow in sync with each other. There was a tremor between them—a flowing current of energy. It was a connection that felt physically uncomfortable to break. Something untouchable that she couldn't imagine being without.

And she knew, by the short beat of time when their eyes locked afterward, that he felt the same way.

If only you had been in my life before Jed Grunder, she thought, looking at him now. *If only you had come along when I still trusted. When I still believed.*

"I know you don't want to go back in there," Gabriel said. "But it's what we have to do. I can't think of another option. I can go in for you, if you just tell me where to find the things we need."

"No," Natalie said. "You're right—someone needs to be keeping watch."

"We do this together," he said, and her heart melted a little at the idea that he felt compelled to fight alongside her, when it was a fight that didn't include him in the least. He'd been in the wrong place at the wrong time, but he was not going to run away.

"Okay," she said, nodding. "But I don't want to leave the mountain. I can't go that far away, knowing Cora is in there. Plus, I don't even know if the Jeep will make it all the way down in this storm. It's worse in the valley."

"We can't stay here, though," Gabriel said. "And we've got to call the police. My phone is still in my room, along with everything else."

"I know. We can try the landline phone, but it's not very reliable in storms. Our first priority is getting the keys. There's another lodge. It's about five miles that way. I'll feel safer there. He won't know where we are, and there'll be other people around. We can call for help from there. Or…or regroup. Or… I don't know. Something."

"Okay," Gabriel agreed, and then he locked eyes with her. "Are you ready?"

She nodded, unable to speak, afraid that what would come out was all of her fears and worries and past trauma. She would never be ready to face Jed Grunder. But she was more than ready to get out of here and let police know where their fugitive was hiding.

They pushed through the snowstorm, cold and shivering, Natalie overly vigilant, afraid that Jed would pop up from behind a bush or a rock or who knew where. He seemed to always have the upper hand on her. And he knew it.

They stole through the woods and came across the lift area on the backside of the terminal, which was obscured from most of the lodge's views. Between their location, the blowing snow and the dusk edging in on them, there was no way Jed could see them from inside the lodge. Or at least that was what Natalie needed to tell herself if she was going to have any courage at all.

Natalie pressed her finger to her lips as they crept up the porch to the front door. She put her hand on the wood, and then remembered the squeak that Cora had been nagging her for weeks to fix. Now she sorely wished she had listened to her friend.

She pushed the door open slowly, slowly, hoping the squeak would blend in with the sound of the wind or be mistaken for the lodge settling. They peered through the open crack, scanning the check-in desk, lobby and dining room, which still flickered with the news. Satisfied that Jed was not going to get in her way of reaching the office, Natalie turned and mouthed to Gabriel, *Stay here*. He nodded, and she stepped into the lodge.

Natalie's legs shook as she crept through the lobby. The most familiar place in the world to her, and now it suddenly felt foreign, full of sinister hiding places where someone could lurk. She wondered how long Jed had prowled around the lodge before making his move. The very thought of him watching her without her knowing made her skin crawl.

How could she have ever misread someone so spectacularly? There was bad intuition and there was completely clueless. She felt like she fell into the completely clueless category. She had been blindsided by him.

Not once, but twice.

The back office was behind the check-in desk. The huge, heavy bookcase that had been a wedding gift for Ruth, handmade by her new husband, stood sentry just outside the office door. It was her prized possession and still carried many of her books and tchotchkes. Cora dusted it dutifully, and Natalie had read every book on its shelves. They'd left it behind the desk after Ruth died, partly in honor of her, but mostly because it was incredibly heavy, and even together, they could barely budge it.

The little cubby office acted as a place of respite for Cora and Natalie when they'd had enough guest time and needed a quiet moment or a lunch break or to make a phone call. It was also a catchall for records and extra keys and random important items. Technically, it should have remained locked at all times. But they didn't have a magnetic key to that door— it had been on the agenda for months—and locking and unlocking with a traditional key was a pain, especially when there were so few guests in the lodge. So they left it unlocked.

Cora trusted people.

Natalie went along with it for the sake of ease.

What about Gabriel? Surely you find him trustworthy.

True. He was standing in the doorway, fists clenched, knees bent, at the ready to take on yet another fight if he had to. Natalie wasn't sure how much fight one man could have in him, but she felt confident that, however much fight Jed had in him, Gabriel would have that plus one more.

Was he someone she could trust forever? She didn't know. Was he someone she could trust today? Absolutely.

She gave him one last look—a reassuring nod, even though her entire body was twisted in terrified knots—and then disappeared behind the check-in desk and slipped into the office.

At first she was struck with how normal everything looked. Exactly as she had left it just a few hours earlier. The ice hadn't even melted in her tumbler yet; her soda still looked fresh. Her pen was still lying on a legal pad, a list of to-dos before the storm hit. She hadn't gotten to cross off "check the feeders." Was that just today? It seemed like a lifetime ago.

But when she arrived at her desk, she noticed that something was actually different. Her purse was dumped onto the floor, its contents scattered, her cell phone smashed to bits, as if someone had stomped on it. Not included in the scattered contents were her car keys. She dropped to her knees and picked up the empty purse, stuffing her hand inside, urgently feeling for them, then feeling nothing, tossed the purse aside and searched again among the items on the floor, as if maybe she'd just missed them on first glance.

They weren't there.

Jed had been in here and made sure Natalie and Gabriel couldn't get off of this mountain. *Not true,* she argued with herself. *He made sure* you *couldn't get off of this mountain. Gabriel has a car, too. You just have to get to his keys. If they're in Gabriel's room, Jed surely hasn't gotten to them. Unless…well, unless he found the other master key.*

With shaking fingers, Natalie frantically punched in the access code on the safe beneath her desk. She got the numbers wrong the first time, so took a deep breath and tried again. She'd opened this safe a million times; it wasn't like she suddenly didn't know how to do it. The second time through, she went slower, and the door popped open. Inside was the spare master key card, which she palmed immediately.

They would get up to Gabriel's room, grab his keys, get back down to his car and continue the plan as normal. Jed may be brutish and violent and murderous and strong, but he couldn't outsmart Natalie; she was sure of it.

As she stood, stuffing the key card into her back pocket, she was startled by a sudden movement out of the corner of her eye, followed by the office door slamming shut. Jed Grunder stood against the wall; he'd been hiding behind the door the entire time.

She'd been so focused on her spilled purse, she'd never checked the door. *He'd* outsmarted *her.*

He held up her Jeep keys, letting them dangle from his index finger.

"Looking for these?"

Natalie froze as Gabriel hit the other side of the door, jiggling the doorknob and pounding the wood, screaming Natalie's name. Her brain raced for a way out of this situation, but she'd said it herself—if someone came into the office behind her, the only way out was through them. She couldn't get through Jed. But still, she could not give up. Maybe she could talk her way out. She had to at least try. She'd never really tried just talking to him. After all, once upon a time, conversation between them was easy. So easy, she'd thought maybe there was something between them.

And, right now, conversation seemed to be the only tool she had at her disposal.

"You don't have to do this," she said, making sure her voice didn't shake and bely the calmness she was trying to portray. It didn't even seem to register with Jed that Gabriel was on the other side of the door, trying with all his might to get in. The bangs and thuds against the door had taken on a stalled quality, which let Natalie know that Gabriel had taken to slamming his body against it, hoping to break it down.

"Oh, but I do." Jed regarded the dangling keys as if he were looking at a new specimen of insect under a microscope. "Don't you think it's interesting how our entire relationship began with a set of keys and is going to end with one, as well? It's like it's all come full circle. Circle of life, if you will." He snorted over his own cleverness. "Or circle of death, as the case may be."

"We never had a relationship," Natalie seethed. "You attacked me."

He nodded. "True. What can I say? I was desperate for money. Starving."

He took a step forward, and Natalie took a step back, shaking her head. "You weren't."

"You're a woman of God. It's your job to help me out. It's not my fault that you resisted your faith and I had to get forceful."

"I would have helped you, though," Natalie said, angry tears streaming down her face. *Keep him talking, Natalie. Just keep him talking.* "I didn't know. All you had to do was tell me. All you had to do was ask. I thought we were friends. I would have helped a friend without even thinking about it." Gabriel hit the door again, and the frame splintered, momentarily distracting Jed, who then took another step to recover from his distraction. Natalie backed up again. She knew that she only had about one more step before she would hit the cabinets that lined the wall across from her desk.

"It's also not my fault that you fell down those stairs and bumped your noggin." Jed reached out and thumped Natalie's head on the word *noggin*. "You're so clumsy." He thumped her head again, twice, as he spoke.

Natalie couldn't help the tears now. They ran freely as she seethed. "That's not how it happened. You know it's not."

He pointed at her with a key, taking another step forward. "You see? That's the lie you told in court, too. You made me sound like a bad guy. This all could have been avoided if you'd just let me have the purse. Why'd you fight so hard for that purse? There was only sixteen dollars and two lousy, maxed-out credit cards inside. Your finances were disappointing, Natalie."

Natalie had spent entire therapy sessions, had gone to her pastor, had worked so hard to deal with her own fear and guilt about this very thing. Why had she fought to keep her purse? Why didn't she just let it go, drop her groceries, get to safety? Why did she almost die over a few dollars? If only she'd done something differently, maybe the attack wouldn't have happened. And she would be lying if she said she didn't have the same thought about what was happening now. If only she'd not pressed to have him put away. If only she'd said she didn't remember anything, didn't know her attacker. If only she'd let it go.

She wouldn't be facing Jed Grunder again.

Cora wouldn't be hurt.

Gabriel wouldn't be in danger.

But it would also have been a big lie.

"I'll forget you were ever here," she said. "I won't tell anyone that I saw you. It'll be like it never happened."

His terrible grin grew. He continued as if she hadn't spoken at all. "See? You're stubborn. You don't know your limits. You just had to go and resist. Just like you're doing now. Resisting. Being a big hero. Well, you're about to find out that you're not a superhero."

A louder thump at the door this time, the frame cracking more, distracted Jed. He glanced at the door. Natalie knew this was her moment. But she hesitated. Even a second of hesitation was too long. He turned back to her, shoved the Jeep keys in his pocket, and reached toward her throat with both hands. She'd missed her chance.

"You're just going to make this harder on her!" he yelled. "And you'll be too late anyway! If she'll stop fighting, this will be over in just a few minutes." He took another step, trapping her against the cabinets behind her. "All those years I've spent in prison have been torture, Natalie. Do you know how bad prison is?"

"Please…" She hated that she was reduced to begging.

"No, you don't know. Or maybe you do, and you wanted to torture me. I get that. It's how I'm feeling right now. I want you to experience the pain and agony I've been experiencing thanks to your actions, Natalie."

She shrank away from his touch as far as she could, her mind racing, but finding no way out. Jed was bigger, stronger, and he had the advantage. There was nothing she could do. She realized then that he intended to make the attack at her apartment a blessing compared to this. That attack was over in the blink of an eye, before she really even realized it had begun, and she'd slipped away from consciousness easily.

He wanted to make this a lingering hurt. A long, slow pain.

Jed pressed his hands around her neck and began to squeeze, pushing his thumbs hard against the base of her throat, instantly cutting off air. Natalie slapped and punched, but he kept her at arm's length, and she ended up mostly slapping and punching the air. She tried to scream, but the sound that came out was a strangled croak, and she immediately wished she hadn't wasted the breath.

Gabriel continued throwing himself against the door, the frame splintering and breaking more with every blow. The lights flickered, but Natalie was unsure if it was the wind, or if it was her consciousness flickering out on her.

And then two things happened at once.

Gabriel burst through the door with a loud crack, at the exact moment that the lights blinked out entirely, plunging the office in darkness so complete, Natalie couldn't even see Jed anymore.

But she knew he was there. And in the distraction, his grip had loosened the tiniest bit. Just enough for her to blindly reach forward until her fingers met flesh that she guessed was his face. She hooked them into claws and raked through the flesh as hard as she could.

Jed let out a howl and his hands fell away from her neck. Sucking in a great gasp of breath, she dropped low and barreled through him, shoving him hard in the dark. She could hear the clang and thud of him losing his footing and toppling over the office chair, giving her just enough time to think. She knew this office like she knew the back of her hand, and could picture where he was sprawled on the floor, struggling to right himself in the dark. She quickly wrapped her hands under the lip of her desk, and heaved it on top of him. He let out a grunt and a wheeze, then went silent and still, as she slipped out the door, Gabriel right behind her.

"Help me with this," she said, as she moved to the far side of Ruth's bookcase. At first, it didn't budge, like every other time she'd tried to move it, but when Gabriel appeared next to her and gave it a heave, it scooted a couple of inches. She opened her mouth to tell Gabriel that they just needed to jam the massive bookcase in the doorway, make it impossible—or at least really difficult—for Jed to get out. But she didn't need to tell him. He already knew.

He threw one hip forward, and used his shoulder to swivel the shelf so the books were facing the office, the shelf blocking the door. *In the morning, that shoulder is going to be murdered,* she thought, and then shook away the immediate following thought: *In the morning, we could all be murdered.*

Inside the office, Jed was stirring. There was a great metallic clang of the chair hitting against something, followed by a bellow.

"Okay, now. Push," Gabriel said.

They both leaned into the shelf and shoved, tapping into muscle reserves that Natalie didn't even know existed. The bookcase tilted, then wobbled, and then, with a wooden grinding noise against the hardwood floor, it toppled. The avalanche of books sounded like thunder hitting the walls and floor, and had Jed not let out the most satisfying cry of fear and frustration, Natalie might have been sad to think of the damage done to Ruth's shelf and beloved books.

The shelf, wider than the doorway, was wedged tight—impossible for one person to move—and just to be sure, Gabriel hurled the two front desk stools on top of it, blocking Jed from being able to crawl out over the top. Or at least slowing him down. The bookcase was a temporary solution, but Natalie didn't need Jed to be trapped forever. She only needed him to be trapped long enough for them to do what they needed to do.

"Outside?" Gabriel asked.

Natalie shook her head. Her hand snaked to her back pocket and pulled out the master key that she'd grabbed from the safe.

"Follow me," she said, and turned toward the stairs.

Natalie was tough. Gabriel had never seen anyone so tough. And thank goodness, given that he had been so busy guarding her from outside the office, he never even considered that Jed could have been inside, hiding behind the door. It was the oldest hide-and-go-seek trick in the world, and they had fallen for it. If he hadn't gotten into that room, he would have never forgiven himself.

He surprised himself with his intensity in ramming the door. It was as if something in him had snapped, almost as if he were ramming his shoulder against all of the events that had led to him being at the Hideaway in the first place.

Of course Gabriel knew that not everything in life would go smoothly. But finding out about Liane and his best friend had been his lowest moment. He liked to think he'd come out stronger, more willing to challenge himself, more aligned with what was important to him, but he hadn't really had a chance to prove it to himself until Natalie was stuck in that room with a murderer.

In some ways, he felt that maybe he had been called to the Hideaway. He'd felt it while he was on the ledge that very first day, when Natalie had popped out of the woods, and his breath had caught. Because it immediately felt right. Like the question he'd been there to answer had been unequivocally and instantly answered.

He wanted to save Natalie because she didn't need saving. Because she was a fighter. She was who he wanted to be. He wanted to save her because he felt a pull to be with her, to get to know her, to learn what made her tick.

He followed Natalie up the stairs, trying to block

out the enraged bellow of Jed extricating himself
from the office chair that he'd fallen over when Natalie had pushed into him. He would be right behind
them. If Natalie knew her way around the lodge the
way Gabriel suspected she did, losing power might
be the best thing that could happen to them. As long
as he could keep her in his sight.

Which wasn't easy to do when they reached the
top of the stairs. Nothing but closed doors. Not a
window to be found. *It's like being inside a tomb*, he
thought, then shook the thought away, annoyed by
his own bleakness.

As they continued down the hall, Natalie's hand
reached back and grabbed his. He was taken out of
the moment for a second to a place of possibility,
where the two of them were walking hand in hand,
content and casual, a single unit of love and happiness. If only…

"We're going to get your car keys," she whispered.
"Do you know where they are inside your room?"

He did. Right next to his wallet on the side table.
Weird, how this had all started with him locking himself out of his room on his search for more cookies.
What might have happened if he hadn't done that?
Would he have been able to get them down the mountain to safety right away with his keys so handy in his
front pocket, just like they usually were? Or would
Natalie have been chased down by two men instead of
one, been easily overpowered and been killed, before
he even realized anything was happening?

Thank you, God, he thought. *For letting me be there.*

He didn't want to be in this position, but if he was going to be, he wanted it to be with Natalie. He wanted to be there for her.

He nodded, and even though he knew that she couldn't see him, she plunged forward as if she'd somehow heard him.

"We can call the police while we're in there," he said. "For Cora."

But he knew Jed was not going to let a bookshelf hold him back forever. And he knew the longer they stayed in a room, the more time they gave Jed to work his way free and catch up. The last thing they needed was him breaking down a door just as Gabriel had done and trapping them inside. What they needed more than anything was distance. Safety.

They inched down the hallway, each of them breathing shallowly, treading lightly on the soft carpet, Gabriel running one hand along the wall to guide him.

He felt Natalie stop and stiffen, and he bumped into the back of her.

"What?" he asked.

"I heard something," she whispered.

He craned his neck and slowed his breathing. All he could hear was Jed's tantrum. "It's good. It means he's still trapped."

"No." He felt her arm move as she pointed down the hallway. "It's coming from down there."

They quieted, and this time, Gabriel did hear it— the shush of someone moving. More of an interruption in the air than an actual sound.

"John," he said, even though he knew that the sound was coming from in front of them rather than above. "He's probably just trying to get loose." Gabriel turned his eyes upward, as if he could see who was moving along the floor by looking through the ceiling.

"Right," Natalie said. "But it sounds like..."

There was another sound, something like a groan.

Even in the dark, he felt Natalie's fear as she tensed next to him, and edged ever so slightly toward the door, her hand working behind her, reaching with the key card to find the lock.

"What?" he asked. "Do you see...?"

But even as he said it, he saw it himself. Two dots, glowing in the dark as they moved forward. Natalie had talked about this on their first conversation together. What they were hearing wasn't the sound of some*one* moving, but some*thing*. Those weren't two glowing dots; they were eyes.

"Mountain lion," he said, or maybe just thought. His mouth dried up, and it could have been nothing more than an exhale that came out. Either way, he knew that Natalie was already well aware of what was coming at them. "It must have gotten in when the door was left open."

"Handle," Natalie breathed, the word just barely audible as she inched farther back, her key-holding hand searching, searching for the sensor.

The dots moved steadily forward, and the groan that they'd heard a moment before turned into a growl.

Gabriel wasn't sure if his eyes were deceiving him, or if he saw a line of sharp teeth appear under the dots.

"Handle," she said again, more urgently.

His arm felt leaden. He didn't want to budge, lest the movement spring the mountain lion into action. But he also knew that not moving meant not getting away, and every second that he allowed the animal to get closer mattered. He reached back and gripped the door handle. He pushed it down, but the door didn't budge.

"Come on, come on," Natalie whispered, as the key card, shaking in her hands, scraped the door, the doorknob, and the metal frame, landing everywhere but the sensor. "I'm trying."

"It's okay," Gabriel said. "We're okay." He had locked on to the glowing dots and felt a bit mesmerized. His entire body was electric and taut. A part of him knew this was going to be the end for him, and he was okay with it. He was right with God, and he felt a kinship with the mountain lion, certain that his death would be merciful in that at least it wouldn't be carried out with malice, but just with an understanding that this is how the food chain works. He was struck with an awareness that humans made things too complicated for themselves. And then complained when life was complicated. It was all really quite simple when it came down to it.

As if it understood what he was thinking, the mountain lion's snarl drew itself deeper, its fangs glistening. He couldn't see the cat's body well in the dark, but he imagined it hunched down, back end tense and wiggling, ready to launch.

Gabriel heard a tick and shush of plastic, followed by Natalie's urgent whisper. "Oh, no. I dropped it."

That was not good. Gabriel glanced and could barely see the silhouette of the card on the floor in front of the door.

"I don't want to startle it," she whispered. "I'm afraid movement will startle it."

Gabriel thought for a second, swallowed and made a decision. "I'll shield you," he said.

"No."

"It'll be okay. We'll move quickly."

"Gabriel."

"It'll be okay," he repeated earnestly, and he really felt it—regardless the outcome, everything would be okay. "On the count of three. One. Two."

"I don't like this."

"We don't have a choice. If we stay here, it will attack both of us. If I step in front of you, it will only attack me."

"And then what? I listen to you die right outside the doorway?"

He swallowed. He didn't have an answer for that, and he would be the first to admit the mental image made him run cold with fear. The cat slowly moved one foot forward, crouching lower, its growl louder. There was no time for mental images.

"It's now or never. One. Two. Three." Gabriel took a swift step forward and in front of Natalie, who whipped around and crouched. In one swoop, she picked up the key, laid it against the sensor and pushed the door handle down.

Just as the mountain lion lunged forward with a sharp cry.

Chapter Eight

Natalie practically threw herself into the room, but fortunately she had the wherewithal to grab the back of Gabriel's shirt as she hurtled through the doorway. The two of them landed on the soft carpet floor. They quickly untangled themselves and used their feet to slam the door closed. At nearly the same time, the cat thudded against the other side, its claws scraping the wood.

After a stunned moment, Natalie collapsed backward on the floor and closed her eyes, desperately trying to slow her breathing, her heart hammering in her chest. She was pretty sure that she was existing only on adrenaline at this point. *If we make it out alive, we will both need to sleep for a hundred days*, she thought.

She glanced to her side. There was a single window in the room, and the curtains were pulled back, allowing in the gray haze of the storm outside. Unlike in the hallway, she could see Gabriel's shadowy figure. He, too, was lying back on the floor catching his breath. But his eyes were open, and he was slowly rolling his shoulder and balling and flexing his right hand.

"You…didn't have…to do that," Natalie said between breaths.

"Yes, I did," he said.

"You could have been killed. Mountain lions are no joke."

He shrugged. "If it was going to be both of us or one of us, I would rather it only be one. And I should be that one. I wanted to protect you."

"Well, then, thank you." Natalie stared at his profile, wondering who on earth this brave man was, and how he ended up in her life. "You're pretty banged up. And that's with what I can actually see in this light. You're probably even worse than I know."

"You should see the other guy." He winked at her and grinned, but it turned into a grimace as he tenderly touched his jaw. "John can throw a punch. I'll give him that."

Natalie pulled herself up on one elbow and looked him over. There were purple bruises sprouting high up on his cheek. His chin was scraped and seeping blood and there was a thin line cut right above his eyebrow. He touched it and hissed through his teeth. Natalie gently pulled his hand away and studied it.

"I'm so sorry that you got caught up in this."

He studied the scrapes on his knuckles as he flexed and released his hand. One knuckle was visibly swollen. "This? Eh, it's nothing. A normal Friday night."

"It's Sunday."

They paused, then both chuckled.

"How can we be laughing right now?" Natalie asked, her laugh threatening to make an abrupt turn to tears. "There's a killer trapped in my office, and a hungry mountain lion prowling the hallways in the dark. And I don't have the foggiest idea how we're still alive."

"You can't make this up," Gabriel said. "We laugh because it's so outlandish. Who would expect this?"

"But my best friend is up there, and it's definitely not funny," Natalie said, staring at the ceiling. "I hope she's alive. I need her to still be alive." She stood up, every muscle in her body wanting to stay down. "I've got to call the police."

She went to the side table and picked up the phone, her shaky fingers punching in 911. It rang only once before a dispatcher picked up. Relief flooded Natalie; she heard the voice of the operator on the other end, but not the words. The ringing in her ears was too loud. She let everything out in one relieved gust.

"We need help. The Snowed Inn Hideaway. The fugitive—the one that you're looking for—Jed Grunder. He's here. And his brother, too. John. John Grunder is his name. I didn't recognize him at first, but he brought Jed into the lodge and they're after us. They're trying to kill us."

"Slow down. You said a fugitive?"

Natalie forced herself to concentrate. "Yes. The one who's escaped from Wyoming State Penitentiary. He's been on TV? I'm the reason he's there, and he escaped to find me and kill me. He's here and he's hurt my friend. I don't know—she could be dead. And we're next. He's after us."

"Who's 'us'?"

Natalie glanced over at Gabriel, who had pulled himself to sitting, his head hanging between his knees. He looked exactly as spent as she felt. "There's another guest. He's helping me. We have Jed trapped in my office, but he's trying to get out. And his brother is upstairs…tied up. And there's a mountain lion prowling around. And we've lost power. We really need help up here."

Natalie could hear the click of computer keys in the background as the officer took down her notes. She could only imagine how all of this sounded to a stranger. She wondered if the police would think this is a prank phone call.

"I know this sounds crazy," she said. "But I promise you I'm not crazy. I own the Snowed Inn Hideaway. I was attacked by Jed Grunder years ago and I helped put him in prison."

"I understand, and we have someone on the way. Does he have any weapons?"

"Not that we've seen, no."

"Okay, and you said that your friend is hurt? You need ambulance service, as well?"

Natalie felt tears brimming as she thought about poor Cora up in that room all alone. Did she think she'd been abandoned? Did she think she was the only one left in the lodge? Obviously, this was the first dispatch had heard of what was going on here, so Cora didn't make any 911 calls from her room. Too hurt to pick up the phone. Or, worse, she was gone, and it was too late for phone calls anyway.

"Yes, I don't know what's wrong because I couldn't get close enough to her. But she looked pretty badly hurt."

The operator paused for so long, Natalie thought maybe they'd been disconnected. But the operator came back, concern lacing her voice. "Where did you say you are again?" she asked.

"The Snowed Inn Hideaway."

"The ski resort?"

"Yes, ma'am."

The operator made a doubtful noise. "It might be a while before anyone can get up there. The roads are completely shut down. Are you in a safe place?"

"We're in a locked room, yes. But the power is out. It's going to get cold in here. I can't get to the generator. Not with that cat roaming around." She'd been too amped up on adrenaline to really notice that there was already a slight chill in the air, but now it was all she noticed. The lodge was old and drafty, and the furnace sometimes had some difficulty keeping up. Cora had been after her to have it replaced. It was on Natalie's to-do list. With no furnace at all, it was going to be even less time before they would start seeing their breath when they talked.

"Any way you can get out of there?"

"We're trying. We've got a car."

"What kind of car?"

Natalie glanced out the window, which overlooked

most of the east side of the lodge—the parking lot side. Had she known that Gabriel was…well, that he was Gabriel, she would have given him a room on the west side, which looked out at the birdbaths and feeders and sweet, hungry Felix. There were only four cars in the lot—the Jeep, Cora's beat-up Corolla, which she hardly ever took anywhere, and two sedans.

"Small," she said. "Small car."

"Honey, that's not gonna make it down the mountain. I'm telling you, the roads are treacherous. They're completely closed. We've got someone on their way. But, again, you need to find safety for a while. If you're safe in that room, stay there for now."

"But Cora…"

"Stay put," the dispatcher repeated.

"Yes, ma'am, of course. Thank you."

By the time Natalie finished her phone call and hung up, Gabriel had gotten up and moved to the bathroom, where he was leaning over the sink, trying to get a look at his face in the mirror, but it was too dark to see.

She went to him, grabbed a washcloth off the towel rack and wet it.

"They're on their way," she said. "Come out here to the window so I can see you."

"Can they get here?" he asked doubtfully.

"They're trying, but it may be a while. Here." She swiveled the office chair to face him, and he sat. She began dabbing at the cuts on his face with the cloth. "In the meantime, we're safe in here and Cora is safe in her room."

Sitting at his desk, Natalie couldn't help noticing that Gabriel's laptop was still open from before he had come downstairs looking for more cookies. It rested on a lock screen that featured Gabriel in much happier times, standing between a man and a woman, his arms around the waists of each. A beautiful woman. Of course. Why would she assume that a man as intriguing and handsome as Gabriel wouldn't be taken?

Natalie wasn't prepared for the pang of disappointment and jealousy that she felt. The woman in the photo looked really happy and comfortable with Gabriel, her arm snaked around his shoulders.

She wondered if this woman knew what Gabriel was capable of. If she knew that he was strong and that he could fight and that he was willing to do whatever it took to save two strangers from very scary men.

She was sure the woman had no idea he was in trouble right now, and wondered if she would be proud of him if—no, *when*—they made it out of this situation.

She wondered, despite herself, if that woman deserved Gabriel.

She felt her cheeks flush, frustrated with herself for the things she was thinking. What did she care about his relationship with this woman? He wasn't Natalie's, and even if he wasn't taken, he still wouldn't be Natalie's. Because Natalie didn't want it that way. She couldn't trust her own instincts when it came to men, and this was just one more example of that.

The man she'd been falling for throughout this whole ordeal was taken, and she didn't even know.

Foolish. Once again. As if she would never learn.

Or, as if you're pulled to this man, and you can't deny it. She supposed she couldn't. That, even through the fear and the running, that same connection she'd felt with him the first time she met him on the ledge, was still there. And getting stronger.

Gabriel winced, and she realized she'd pressed a little too hard against the cut above his eyebrow.

"Sorry," she said. Fresh blood began to seep from the wound. "You're probably going to need stitches there."

"Well, that will only add to my rugged good looks," he quipped.

Natalie tried to laugh, but the problem was she did think he had rugged good looks, and it was as if he'd seen inside her thoughts when he said that. Her laugh dried in an embarrassed clearing of her throat.

"Sorry," he mumbled. "I know none of this is funny. It does make problems that we had before look small now." He gestured toward a legal pad on the desk right next to his computer.

Her eyes trailed to the pad: "Pros and Cons."

Interesting. She knew he was wrestling with a decision. This was likely what he was thinking about when he was overthinking on the ledge.

"'Pro,'" she read aloud. "'No more surprises. Con. Expensive.'" Her forehead creased as she puzzled over that one. "'Con. Farther away from the mountain. Pro. She would be a distraction, anyway.'"

"Um," he said, shifting in discomfort, but he didn't seem to know what else to say.

"She's beautiful," Natalie said, trying to make things less uncomfortable and only seeming to make them more uncomfortable in the process. "I can see why you would want to spend time with her here."

He ducked away from the washcloth and turned so he could see Natalie better. "She who?"

Natalie gestured toward the laptop. "Is the woman in that picture not the she on the list?"

He glanced at the computer screen and an incredulous smile spread across his face. "My sister?"

"That's your sister?"

He nodded and disturbed the touch pad to wake up the computer. The photo popped up again, and Natalie realized she should have seen the full context. There was definitely more of a camaraderie between the three of them than anything romantic. Once again, she had misread a situation. *Your mind shows you what you're afraid of,* she thought, remembering the words of the therapist that she'd seen after the attack, when she was dealing with constant fear. "That's my brother-in-law, Daniel, and my sister, Grace." He clicked around until he pulled up another photo from what looked like the same day. They were in a backyard, balloons and streamers strung along a privacy fence, an older man standing at a barbeque grill, a woman sitting in a lawn chair waving at the camera. There were palm trees in the background. "That's my mom and dad. It was my niece's fifth birthday party."

"Oh," Natalie said, now feeling mortified for how

she'd overreacted about the lock screen photo, even if he didn't know what her reaction had been.

"Grace is great—don't get me wrong—but she is definitely not the one who would distract me on this mountain."

"Oh," Natalie said again. She couldn't seem to muster anything else in her humiliation.

So he helped her out. "You're the she. You're the distraction."

Natalie's eyes flicked up, a feeling of warmth blooming inside of her instantly—part self-consciousness, part something else that she couldn't identify.

He reached over and gently took the washcloth out of her hand. Her fingers were numb and let it slip away easily. Just as gently, he held her fingers in his, rubbing his thumb over her knuckles. "As soon as I met you, I knew I would be coming back. And not because of the towels or the French toast or the hospitality or the ledge or the animals. I think you're beautiful. And you're strong. And fearless. Captivating."

Natalie ducked her head. "I'm not those things."

"You are." He used his finger to tilt her chin so that she was looking at him once again. "You're all of those things. And it would be a distraction. It already was. As soon as I met you, I could hardly stop thinking about you."

"You don't know the half of it," she said, and suddenly she hated the way she walked around feeling ruined all the time. All thanks to the man currently attempting to pound his way out of her office. She wanted to be the things that Gabriel was saying she was, but she never would be those things.

"Neither do you," he said.

"But I'm also a con," she said, pulling her hand away and gesturing to the pad. "Or a pro that is actually a con."

He grinned sadly. "You are."

She picked up the cloth and took it back to the bathroom. Out of habit, she rinsed it out, squeezed it dry and hung it over the shower rod. No, maybe not habit—optimism. This would end and she and Cora would still be around to make sure that cloth wasn't permanently bloodstained.

But she was also wasting time. Absorbing what Gabriel said.

She stared at herself in the mirror. She was just as beat-up as he was. She was disheveled. She looked shell-shocked, terrified, tense, jumpy. Dried blood dripped down the sides of her face, a dark gash on her forehead, surrounded by pink bruising.

She did not look captivating.

Probably because she didn't want to be anyone's captive.

She turned off the water, turned off her curiosity and her blooming feelings of love and walked back into the bedroom.

Gabriel had serious doubts about the police arriving. He heard no sirens, no approaching vehicles. He only heard the sigh of the wind against the lodge, and the faint, persistent thuds of Jed Grunder demanding release.

Keep trying, buddy, he thought to himself, and then revised. *Actually, stop trying.*

He would prefer to leave Jed in there until the police arrived to take him away. Gabriel was spent, and he felt like he needed time to think.

He felt guilty about calling Natalie a con.

But she was. He couldn't help it. Yes, he was drawn to her. In fact, he was drawn in a way that he hadn't felt since Liane. But that was exactly the problem. He'd promised himself that he wouldn't be drawn like that again. Ever. Liane was the first and last. Or, at least, that was what he thought.

So, yes, the fact that he wanted to forget all about what had happened with Liane when he met Natalie made Natalie a definite entry on the con list. She could derail not just his plans but derail his entire life if he let her. He didn't want to let her.

He knew he had said the wrong thing by the way she took the washcloth to the bathroom and stayed there for a minute. He kicked himself for hurting her, yet at the same time, he was only trying not to hurt himself. Or trying not to hurt her worse in the long run, when it was fully evident that this just wouldn't work out between them.

That was a tough hurt to swallow. A tough hurt to get over.

Tougher than never having loved her at all?

That, he couldn't say for sure.

When Natalie reemerged from the bathroom, she

looked different. More resolved, somehow, and Gabriel even more sorely wished he had said something different. Or maybe nothing at all. Maybe if he'd just let her believe that Grace was his betrothed, it would have spared both of them.

They were going to be stuck here for a while. He had to say something. Had to break the ice.

"Career change," he said, grabbing the legal pad and holding it up for her to see. "That's what the list is about. I actually told Cora about it before all this happened. I'm good at private investigation. A little too good. But I think I want out. I want something more. Considering maybe law school. Rather than just outing the bad guys, I want to be the guy who makes sure they pay for their crimes."

"What does that mean, a little too good?"

"I...found someone. Someone I shouldn't have."

"Oh," she said, alarm crossing her face.

"It broke up a relationship. And a friendship, too, actually. It was pretty destructive."

Her forehead creased. "I mean, aren't private investigators there to find out the truth?"

He nodded. "We are. But sometimes the truth hurts. Sometimes it hurts too much. It gets...personal."

Natalie sat on the edge of the bed. She seemed to understand that Gabriel meant it had gotten personal for him. He wanted to let her in on his hurt, but at the same time, he wanted to keep her at arm's distance. The more he let her in, the harder it would be to let her go.

"But, you know, career changes are big. So I feel like I can't just jump into it. That's why I'm making the list."

"I get that," she said. "I made a huge change when I came up here. But I didn't make a list. I had one big pro, and no con would be big enough to overpower it. I was hiding." She paused and glanced at the door where Jed's voice was still floating. "A lot of good that did me. Apparently, I wasn't hiding well enough."

"That's what I don't want to be doing, though," Gabriel said. "Hiding. I want to make sure I'm making the change for the right reason."

"And are you?"

He studied his list. It was short. The top entry on the pro list was that he just plain didn't want to do this anymore. He sighed. "I don't know. I want to bring good into the world, you know? And I think maybe what I've been doing is just…contributing to the bad. My findings cause heartbreak and fighting."

"The heartbreak and fighting would still be there even if you weren't doing this, though," she said. "You're not causing it. You're just…"

"Exposing it," he said. "And that's the part I don't like anymore. There's no closure. For anyone. Not even me. Instead of just exposing people, I want to be the one to bring justice for the people left behind. Does that make sense?"

Natalie nodded. "Totally."

"I…" Gabriel paused. He was sure he just heard a voice. Not Jed's, which was still going nonstop, but someone else. Very muffled, very faint. "Do you hear that?"

Natalie's forehead creased as she glanced at the door and leaned toward it just slightly. She shook her head. "All I hear is Jed."

Gabriel set the legal pad back on the desk and strained to listen. All he could make out was Jed's yell. "Yeah, that must be it," he said.

But, seconds later, he heard it again. A muffled voice that now sounded as if it had split into multiple voices. And it wasn't coming from the office.

It was coming from outside.

And it wasn't Jed, but the voices of two women.

He jumped up, his wobbly legs protesting against the sudden movement, and placed his hands on the window. He leaned forward, pressing his forehead against the glass. The voices sounded closer here.

Natalie must have finally heard it, too, because she made a small noise that sounded something like alarm mixed with dread and joined him at the window.

The parking lot was empty, but the voices were coming from the front of the building. They both turned their heads so that their cheeks were pressed to the glass. Natalie's wild hair brushed against Gabriel's neck, tickling it.

"There," she said. "That's…oh, no. That's the mom and daughter that were staying here. The…the Carringtons." Sure enough, Gabriel recognized the two women who were approaching the lodge, bickering. Their coats and hats were covered with snow, as were the bottom halves of their pantlegs. They'd been among the last to leave the lodge, neither of them wanting to cut their girls' weekend short. Their footprints stretched down the drive as far as Gabriel could see, an arc of divots leading all the way up the front walk.

"What on earth are they doing back?" Natalie slapped the window with the palm of her hand. "Don't come in here!" she shouted, but they didn't appear to hear her. She pounded the window with more vigor, and Gabriel joined her.

"Hey!" he yelled, and, very briefly, the two women paused. They looked around a little, but never looked up, and then went back to their journey to the front door.

The closer they got to the lodge the harder and faster Natalie and Gabriel banged the window, to the point where Gabriel feared they would break it. But it was to no avail. The women pressed forward, oblivious. Natalie spun and leaned against the glass, tipping her head back and closing her eyes in exasperation.

"What do we do now?" she asked. "They're going to get hurt. Why did they come back?"

Gabriel didn't get the chance to answer.

"Hello? Is there anyone here?" Gabriel heard from the direction of the lobby. "The lights are out—oh! What is...? Mom, there's someone trapped in there! Sir? Hello? Are you okay? How on earth did that happen?"

Natalie's eyes flew open. "No," she said. "No, no, no. Don't let him out...don't let him out!" She practically flew to the door, her hand outstretched to grasp the doorknob.

Gabriel grabbed her wrist before she could get there. "What are you doing?"

She gestured toward the door. "They're going to let Jed out. He'll kill them."

"Have you forgotten? There's a mountain lion out there. It'll kill you."

"And if they let Jed out, he will kill me. And, besides, I can't let them just wander in when there's a mountain lion in here, either."

"But we need a plan."

"The plan is to get them out of here," Natalie said, wrenching her wrist out of his hand. She went back to calling for the two women. "Get out! Don't let him out! He's dangerous!"

Gabriel launched in front of her and pressed himself against the door. "I can't let you just go out there. We've come this far together, and we will end this together. If you go out there, I'm going with you. We need a plan. If we go out there without one, and get killed, it won't help them at all."

Natalie paused, and then slumped. "Okay. You're right. What should we do?"

"Get them up here for now," he said. "And once we're all in here, we can decide how we're going to get out of here. Maybe there'll be more strength in higher numbers. This could be a good thing." *Or they can drag us down, and we'll all be dead,* he thought.

There were more muffled shouts, and the thud of heavy things hitting the floor downstairs. Natalie's eyes flicked to the door. She licked her lips. "Are they trying to help him get out?"

He nodded. "Sounds like it."

"We've got to move fast. We've got to stop them. How are we going to get them up here?"

Gabriel took a breath. He was exhausted and sore, but his body was building energy. Ramping itself back up. His muscles tensed, and he could feel it all the way up his neck. He knew there was really only one option. "I'll go get them," he said.

"I'll go with you. You said it yourself. If one of us goes, we both go."

He shook his head. "I was wrong. Someone has to stay here to open the door in case the mountain lion is still out there. You stay and listen for us. Be ready to let us in as soon as you hear us get to the top of the stairs. I don't know how fast they can be, but I'll whisk them away and bring them right up here."

Natalie seemed torn. She licked her lips again. "It's risky."

"I know."

"You'll have to be careful."

He spread his hands across his chest. "I'm always careful." But then winced when he hit a sore spot on his sternum. He wanted to leave her with positivity, just in case…well, just in case. But she was too worried. She didn't even crack a grin.

"Wait. Here. Follow me." She hurried into the bathroom. He followed and watched as she pulled the towels off of the wrought iron towel bar and tossed them to the ground. She wrapped both hands around the rod and gave a mighty tug. It pulled away from the wallboard just a tiny bit. She wrenched the rod up and down, loosening the screws that was holding it onto the wall. Finally, it popped off, sending her stumbling backward into the sink. She gazed at the holes left in the wall for a half a moment, and then held the rod out to him. "Take this. Just in case."

He took the bar from her and felt the weight of it in his hand. This woman was strong, and once again he was struck with the knowledge that she didn't need anyone to save the day for her. She could save her own day.

"Great idea," he said. "Thanks."

"Also, there is a closet by the front door. On the floor of that closet is a box. Inside the box there should be a couple of flashlights. I haven't checked the batteries in a while, but hopefully one will still work."

"Okay. Sure. I'll check."

"You sure you don't want me to go?" she asked. "I know exactly where everything is. I can get to it in the dark with no problem."

He shook his head. "We haven't had the easiest time with getting into safe rooms. You're the insurance policy. I'll be okay. I promise."

She gave a quick nod—his cue to go.

He returned to the door and opened it a tiny crack, his fist squeezing the towel rod. He half expected to see the mountain lion still sitting in the hallway and tensed his arm to ready it for a swing. It reminded him of all the times he'd had to creep around angry dogs and curious cats in his career. And one very feisty rooster. He almost chuckled, remembering how the rooster had pecked at his ankles and caused him to fall into a patch of poison ivy. Private investigation was hardly the glamorous job it was sometimes portrayed as on TV.

"Is it out there?" Natalie whispered.

He shook his head. "Not that I can see."

"Be careful, it could be hiding in a shadow."

Yes, he was aware of that possibility, and he didn't like the image of the wild cat popping out at him as he passed by. "Got it."

"Be fast."

He felt her hand squeeze his shoulder, a message of confidence and fear and comfort all in one. It was exactly what he needed to step out into the hallway. He looked back at her one time, and gave a quick nod meant to convey that he had this under control, and she could shut the door.

She answered his nod with her own, and let the door click shut.

Chapter Nine

Natalie paced the room while she waited for Gabriel to come back. The instant he left, it felt like a thousand years had gone by. She alternately shut all sound out or strained to hear him come to a violent end at the paws of the mountain lion. She didn't want to hear it if that happened. After all, hearing it wouldn't make it stop.

She thought about what would happen when he got back with the Carringtons. How they would get out of this mess. If the women were back at the lodge, it must have meant that their car didn't make it down the mountain. Which was not a positive sign about getting the police here anytime soon. Furthermore, they'd left in an SUV; if Natalie was right, and the SUV couldn't traverse the mountain in the storm, there was basically no chance that they would make it down in Gabriel's little sedan. There had to be another way.

They could hide. Wait it out until the police arrived. The room was comfortable and, for now, warm enough. *But Cora...*

She tried not to think about the fireplace downstairs, and how she and Cora would sit in front of it when the power went out. Cora would often bring supplies for s'mores, which she always seemed to have on hand. It was a nod to their mentor, a habit they'd formed by her side and never let go.

Ruth loved nothing more than a good, dark day without power. She adored wrapping up in a heavy quilt, sitting in front of the fire, eating gooey marshmallows, and telling them stories. Her childhood days spent in the valley, always wondering what mysterious things lived in the mountains. She talked about meeting her husband, about falling in love. About losing two babies to miscarriage, and then losing her husband to a car accident, and moving away from the valley, making the mountain her heart's focus.

She told them how to run a successful business, about how customers came back if they felt not just welcomed but appreciated. How there was a fine line between good service and hovering. Natalie and Cora would sit side-by-side, listening, sometimes giggling, sometimes sighing in comfort, Cora's head on Natalie's shoulder or vice versa.

Natalie sank onto the edge of the bed. *Ruth, please, if you're there...if you have any way of helping from up there...please keep Cora alive.*

At some point early on, it became clear to Natalie that she and Ruth were both in such a remote location for a reason. Both were hiding in some way—

Natalie from Jed and Ruth from loss. But Cora never volunteered why she was there. Why she had no family. Why she had no reason to stay on flat ground below. She never left the lodge. Never took a vacation or went to a funeral or spent a week with family. If Natalie pressed her, she changed the subject, and eventually Natalie just came to accept that Cora had her own hurt, and that it was too personal to divulge. To anyone.

When Ruth died and left the lodge to Natalie, Natalie was sure that Cora would move on to bigger and better things. But she didn't. She stayed with the Hideaway. She stayed with Natalie. She was in it for the long haul. She just probably never thought the long haul would end so soon and at the hands of a murderer.

"And, Ruth?" she said aloud, turning her eyes toward the ceiling. "Help me figure out how to get us out of this mess. Cora's counting on me."

She glanced at the clock. Gabriel had been gone for less than five minutes. It felt like five years. She got up and resumed pacing, which took her back to the window. The prints that the ladies had left behind were snowed over already. This storm was showing no signs of letting up.

She sighed and pressed her hands to the table, accidentally leaning on the yellow legal pad. Pros and cons. Pros and cons.

Con: I'm good at what I do.
Pro: Too good.

Pro: No longer carry the burden of providing closure to suffering people.
Con: No longer using my skills to provide closure to suffering people.

He'd written in the margin, *Is that really true, though? Different closure.*

The final entry on the list:

Pro: Can finally let go.
Con:

He'd written no con to cancel out that pro. Did that mean he'd come down on the side of going to law school? That he was ready to finally let go of the past he was holding on to? What must that feel like?

She was thinking too much. Gabriel wasn't hers, so why did she care so much about his decision? *I think you're beautiful. And you're strong. And fearless. Captivating.*

But I'm also a con.

You are.

She gave a grunt of frustration and pushed away from the table. What was taking so long?

The sound of Jed yelling and pounding had subsided, but then, as she listened, picked up again, only with more urgency than before.

Gabriel must have made it downstairs.

It was only a matter of time now. Which was good.

She felt cold and unmoored without him here.

She needed him.

* * *

Gabriel was certain he heard the shift and shush of the cat, and beyond that was the feeling of being watched. Sensing the presence of others was a skill he'd developed for his own safety. For this reason, he took each step slowly, barely scooting one foot in front of the other, fist wrapped tight around the towel rod, elbow bent to swing.

He couldn't get the sound of Jed choking Natalie out of his head. Even through the locked office door, he could hear it. That was what spurred him to use even more vigor when slamming against it. Willing it open. When it finally let loose and he stumbled into the office, he had a millisecond before the power went out to see Jed's hands wrapped around Natalie's throat, her grasping and swatting at him, her eyes bugged out with fear and acknowledgment that this was the end for her. He would never get that image out of his mind.

He'd almost lost her.

But I'm also a con.

You are.

Something else had dawned on him as a result of seeing that, though. Jed had no weapon. Why? He was running from prison, sure, but John wasn't. Why hadn't John met them with a gun? Why not end it quickly?

There could be only two reasons that Gabriel could think of:

1. They'd surprised John and Jed in that room, and somewhere in there, a gun was hidden. If Gabriel and

Natalie could get back into that room, they could get their hands on it, and they could be the ones to end things quickly.

2. Jed and John wanted this to be drawn out. They wanted it to hurt.

Either way, Gabriel needed to get back into that room to find out.

The commotion downstairs had gotten less frantic and more organized, as if the two ladies were working together with Jed. His throat bulged with the desire to call out, to tell them to stop. But, again, the fear of spooking the cat kept him silent.

Shush, shush, shush, went his shoes on the carpeted floor as he approached the stairwell, which seemed even darker than the hallway. He squinted to try to glean some light from somewhere—anything!—but ultimately had to go on feel. He inched his foot forward until he felt the edge of the top stair and then took a step down.

He heard something behind him, something moving in the hallway. His heart leaped and he twisted so that his back was against the wall, the rod held in front of him, as he scooted down the stairs sideways.

As he descended the stairs, he began to hear the mother and daughter mumbling as they cooperated on the task of releasing Jed. They had no idea.

"Okay, I've got a lot of the books on this side. How are you doing over there?"

"I've still got a few more. Sir? If we pull, will you be able to push? We just about have you. I think if

we just turn it a little more sideways, it'll drop down
and you can climb over."

"It's really wedged, Mom. I don't know. Oh, wait.
I think it moved a little."

"Keep going, sir. We're almost there. Goodness,
I don't know what happened here, but what a good
thing we came along."

Almost there. That was the last thing anyone needed.
Gabriel gave one last, uneasy look up the stairs, saw
no glowing eyes and quickly ran down the last few.
He heard a light gasp when his feet hit the hardwood
of the lobby.

"Who's there?"

"Hello? Who are you?"

Gabriel wanted to shush them, to call out to them,
but something told him to keep silent. Not to let Jed
know that he was back. It would only fuel Jed's anger.
Let him keep thinking his rescue was imminent. He
held his finger to his lips but knew they couldn't see
him.

"Mom, did you hear someone?"

"Yes, I can see them. Hello? I can see you."

"Say something." The girl's voice was shaky. She
was undoubtedly feeling the way Natalie had earlier—trapped and scared. "Mom, they're holding
something. Are you the person who did this? Hello?"

"Yes," Gabriel heard Jed say from the office. "Yes,
they're very dangerous. Take them down."

"We're armed," the mom said. Her voice was just
as shaky as her daughter's.

Gabriel was pretty sure that they weren't armed.

But they were surrounded by heavy books, and if they wanted to, they could certainly begin throwing those at him. Dodging flying objects in the dark wouldn't be easy.

Gabriel knew that he had to make himself known.

"Yes, I trapped him. He's dangerous. I'm here to help get you to safety," he said. "You should come with me."

"What?" the daughter asked.

"Who are you?" the mom asked at the same time.

Gabriel was closing the distance as quickly as he possibly could. He held the towel rod up in surrender style. Still, he could see their figures as he got closer to them, both of them shrinking back.

"Mom…" the girl whimpered.

Gabriel gave a quick glance backward, searching for the wild cat, but saw only the darkness of the staircase. He had to make a show of being trustworthy. He didn't want to lose his weapon, but he bent and set it on the floor with a soft clink, then stood, hands still up as if in surrender, and closed the distance to the desk. One of them—the girl, he thought—climbed over the toppled bookshelf to be closer to the other.

"I'm safe," he whispered. "I'm with Natalie. The owner."

"What's going on?" Jed said, louder this time. "Hey! Did you leave?" He swore, and the bookshelf shifted, causing both ladies to jump and cling together. "Don't trust them. They're going to hurt you. They'll trap you like they did me."

Gabriel was close enough to see the shapes of their

features, their eyes wide and shiny, their mouths open. He held his hands up higher. "I need you to trust me."

"No way," the girl said, shaking her head and clinging tighter to her mother.

Jed swore again and rattled hard against the bookcase, which shook and shifted a few inches more. Surely at this point, it was barely staying wedged and would soon fall enough for him to scramble past it. The mom glanced toward Jed and then back at Gabriel. "What happened here?" she asked.

Gabriel put his hands down and hurried to the closet by the still-open front door, slipping in a puddle of blown and drifted snow that had melted. He practically dived inside the closet, pawing through hanging coats to get to a box, which he found easily. Inside were what felt like a dozen flashlights. He pulled one out and snapped the button. Nothing. He tossed it aside and tried another. Dead. A third also remained dark.

He was starting to despair that maybe Natalie had been wrong. He thought wryly about the dead flashlights in his own house. That was the irony of flashlights—you rarely needed one, so the batteries were always inevitably drained by the time you did need one. He picked up a fourth and pushed the button.

The light came on.

He nearly cheered.

Instead, he used it to see the other flashlights in the box and rooted around until he found two more that worked.

"Here." He held two flashlights out for them to

take. The ladies looked at each other but didn't move from their spot behind the front desk. He wiggled the lights. "Here. We don't have time."

They looked at each other again, and then must have decided it was safe, because they inched forward, and each took a flashlight from him. He stood, started to shut the closet door, and stopped. There were several jackets and coats in here, along with another box filled with gloves, hats and scarves. He and Natalie had been running around throughout all of this with no protection from the wind and cold. His things were in his room, but presumably Natalie's things were right here. He quickly grabbed a stocking cap and pulled it onto his head, stuffed a pair of gloves into the pocket of one coat and pulled the coat off of its hanger.

"Here," he said once again, holding the coat out toward the mother. "We need to take this up to Natalie."

The mother stared at it for a long moment before slowly taking it. "Tell us what's going on," she said. "Who is in that room?"

"I'll tell you everything when we get upstairs. But what I can tell you right now is the man in that office is very bad, and if he gets out, he will try to kill us. We knocked over the bookshelf to trap him in there, and now we're hiding in my room upstairs."

"Don't listen to him! He's lying to you!" Jed shouted.

"There's also a mountain lion somewhere in the building. Or at least there was. And it wasn't happy. Acting very aggressive."

The daughter gasped and grabbed at her mom's sleeve.

"I've got that little metal rod," he said, pointing at the towel rod that was still on the ground where he'd laid it. "And the room is right at the top of those stairs. Come with me, keep your flashlights on and your eyes open and walk very slowly. If the cat thinks you're charging, you're in big trouble."

The daughter shook her head. "Mom, no. Let's just get out of here. Go back to the car."

"If you go up to that room with him, he will kill you," Jed said. "Think about it. Why is he trying to trap you? He's already trapped me. Don't fall for it."

"Come on, Mom, let's just go."

The mother seemed torn, taking in her daughter's words and Jed's accusations and Gabriel's pleas, and trying to assimilate them into her own thoughts. "We can't get down that mountain," she said. "It's going to be evening soon. If we go back to the car, we'll freeze to death out there, or run into some animal, or who knows what?"

"But we don't know him at all. That guy is right—he's already trapped someone. What if he wants to trap us?"

"We trapped him because he was trying to kill us. He was strangling Natalie. Please, listen to me."

The woman looked at the office. The bookshelf had scooted another couple of inches, and now half of Jed's face was visible above it. He had quieted but was clearly still working busily on moving the shelf. Gabriel had to persuade them to come with him.

"That man…he's a fugitive… I'm sure you've seen him on TV. He attacked a woman who works here. She's hanging on by a thread. We've got to get help for her. Police are on their way. If he gets out of that office, and you're out here, you will be next. I can guarantee it. We don't have time. Let's go," Gabriel said.

The mother and daughter looked at each other uncertainly, and the mother gave the tiniest nod. The daughter let out a little sob and then nodded in response. Gabriel nearly heaved a sigh of relief when they began moving toward him.

Thank you, God. Thank you.

They moved toward the stairs, with Gabriel at the lead, moving slowly, slowly. The beams of their flashlights clawed open their path, and Gabriel felt much more at ease knowing that he would see the mountain lion before hearing it, if it was still around.

The daughter continually whimpered behind him, and he felt bad about her fear. But he knew that Natalie would be able to calm and reassure her, even if she didn't feel calm and reassured herself. He paused at the bottom of the stairs, just to make sure they were still with him. They were, the mother's eyes piercing a plea—or maybe it was a warning—at him: *We will fight back if we have to.*

Jed, understanding that his help had been taken from him when his escape had been oh so close, roared a flurry of hateful insults and threats at them, the sounds of him kicking and shoving at the bookcase growing ever louder and more impatient.

He will get that bookcase moved, Gabriel thought.

It's heavy, but not impossible. Once it's unwedged, he will get out.

We've got to move faster.

He pressed a finger to his lips to remind his travelers that they needed to be quiet, and then began the ascent up the stairs. Thirteen steps, and he would be back to safety, back with Natalie. One, two, three...

Up and up, the flashlight beams bobbing, the daughter's breath hitching, Gabriel's own breath pluming out ahead of him. The lodge was getting colder with no power—something he was trying to avoid acknowledging. He was also trying to avoid acknowledging that Jed was going about his task of busting out of the office wordlessly now, the bangs and scrapes coming from below a concerted, concentrated task.

"Mom, I don't like this," the daughter whimpered. "They say you should never go with someone."

The mother shushed her. "We're going to be fine."

"We're almost there," Gabriel whispered. Eight, nine, ten... His flashlight beam seemed to be getting smaller, narrower as they neared the top of the steps and the hallway both widened and lengthened. He hoped Natalie could hear them coming. He imagined her standing on the other side of the door, her ear literally pressed to it, as she strained for whatever sign she needed to allow herself to pull it open and let them inside.

Eleven.

Twelve.

As he raised his leg to take the final step, he noticed a shadow to his right shift. His breath caught, knowing that the cat had hidden in that corner and was now coming for him.

But what stepped out wasn't the mountain lion.

It was John Grunder.

And he was holding a knife.

He dropped the broken drapery cord at Gabriel's feet. It coiled into a little pile on Gabriel's shoe.

"You need to learn to tie better knots," John said.

"Run!" Gabriel said, and then louder, so Natalie could hear. "Get into the room!"

The two women pushed past him and began pounding on the door, shouting.

Natalie opened the door, wary confusion on her face, just as John swung the knife.

Chapter Ten

Natalie could hardly believe what she was seeing. She was almost stunned into inaction, feeling the two women shove her with their shoulders so they could get inside. They were screaming at her, but the sounds were jumbled, garbled, almost in the background, her periphery, as she took in what was happening in the hallway.

She'd been so focused on Jed, she'd nearly forgotten about John. Yet now that he was standing in front of her—was he holding a knife from her very own kitchen?—she realized he may be the one to be more afraid of. He was bigger than his brother, stronger, and hadn't been living in confinement for the past six years. And seemed equally motivated to see her die, even if it meant he had to get through Cora and Gabriel to make it happen.

Instinctively, she wanted to hold up her hands, as if in surrender. As if that would do any good. As if she only surrendered, they would call it good and leave the Hideaway, let her be.

No. They wouldn't stop until she was dead. They'd said so, and she believed them. And she believed Jed when he said her death wouldn't be quick and pain-less.

And she couldn't even think about what they'd do to Gabriel. And Cora. If she was still alive, would they simply let her slowly die? With this storm, no-body would be coming to the lodge anytime soon, so by the time anyone stumbled upon them, it would be far too late to save anyone.

Besides, John was so focused on Gabriel at the mo-ment, she didn't think he even noticed that she was standing there with her hands up, anyway.

She was tired. Her muscles ached and her body felt sore and weak. She wanted this to be done.

"Don't," she said, but unlike Jed, John wasn't one for talking.

"Get inside, Natalie," Gabriel said. "Don't come out unless I tell you to."

John launched himself into Gabriel, who seemed to be at the ready, knees bent to absorb the blow, hand up to catch the wrist on John's knife-swinging hand. So different from the man who was first attacked in the room where they found Cora, completely un-prepared and instantly knocked down. Gabriel was tough, a quick learner and certainly unafraid to get into the mix when he had to. Maybe this was what was meant by being too good at his job. Maybe just because someone was good at something didn't mean they enjoyed doing it.

Natalie cried out, then pressed a fist to her lips. She couldn't go inside and leave him like this. Still, at the same time, she didn't know how to help him, either. The two men struggled, thudding against the wall next to Natalie, as Gabriel held tight to John's wrist with one hand and swung punches with the other. He landed a few, but no matter how hard he tried to duck away, he was also taking a few, and he was already slowing down. His arm shook, the knife pressing closer and closer to his face.

She could hear the cries of the two women behind her, and feel them press up against her, trying to see what was happening in the hallway. She felt the weight of the door against her shoulder lighten as the mother pulled it open farther to peek out.

"Who is that?" she shrieked, only inches from Natalie's ear. "What's going on here?"

Natalie winced from the ear-piercing sound but didn't respond.

"Is that a knife? He has a knife?"

The daughter screamed, adding to the noise and confusion. Any hope they had of keeping their whereabouts from Jed was for sure gone.

Gabriel grunted and gave an extra push, propelling himself and John away from the wall. The two stumbled, and Natalie thought they were going down, but somehow, they stayed upright and simply slammed against the wall on the other side of the hallway. This time Gabriel was doing the pinning and was repeatedly bashing John's knife-holding hand against the wall. But John held tight.

She had to help.

Somehow, John managed to flip them around and had Gabriel bent backward over the banister, the knife pointed only centimeters above Gabriel's chest. Even in the dark, Natalie could sense Gabriel's struggle. She felt, rather than saw, Gabriel's biceps shaking and straining. She sensed how close the danger was.

And she couldn't help being transported back to that night in her own stairwell. In her flashbacks, it was all over so quickly. He snatched the purse, shoved her down the stairs and came down to finish her off with punches and kicks until she stopped moving.

But watching Gabriel's struggle now, she was transported backward to a different struggle that had once been forefront in her memory and she'd actively worked to push it back.

Oh, thank goodness, it's you. I have all these groceries and I can't get into my...

His eyes. She'd seen it in his eyes before he'd even made a move. The warmth and kindness that she'd been falling for had disappeared, replaced by something cold and empty. She'd already taken a step back before he even reached for her, her gut instinct telling her that something was about to happen, and it would be bad. She'd immediately gotten warm, her entire body tingling with alarm.

What she didn't remember—she had fought him. Had held tight to her purse strap and tugged against him. Had pummeled him with her fists when it looked like he wasn't going to give up.

She had screamed for help.

Hoped someone would come for her.

No one ever did.

She couldn't let that be Gabriel's story, too. She'd been lucky to come out alive, and who was to say that he would also be so lucky?

"Hold the door," she said to the woman standing behind her. The daughter, crying across the room, jumped forward.

"Mom, no! Don't!"

But Natalie didn't have time to convince her. Gabriel was losing steam. John's knife was touching his chest now.

Natalie raced out of the room and down the hallway to the fire extinguisher, too panicked and too focused to notice that the mountain lion had popped out from a shadow, ears back and squatting to pounce. She ripped open the little metal door and snatched the fire extinguisher, then ran back to the stairs. She was going to be too late. She dug deeper and closed the last few steps, raising the extinguisher over her head as she ran.

Gabriel's eyes flicked to her, distracting John, who turned just in time for her to bring the extinguisher down on him. The thud of metal on skin made her recoil. She felt painful reverberation up the entire length of her arms. The extinguisher fell out of her hands and onto the floor, then bumped down the stairs. But she'd done what she'd come to do. John dropped the knife, and his hands flew up to his head. Gabriel quickly kicked the knife toward Natalie, but it wasn't necessary. John reeled backward, and then stumbled forward, overcorrecting, both hands holding his head where Natalie had hit him. He'd turned just enough that he was hovering over the staircase. He lifted a foot as if to navigate the first step. A flight response. But his foot came down on air and he pitched forward.

For a moment, in the dark, it seemed as if he had simply vanished into thin air. But then came the sound of his body hitting the stairs, the grunts of wind being knocked out of him, and, finally, the crack of spindles as he came to rest against them near the bottom. And then, silence.

Natalie realized she was holding her breath and let it loose. Gabriel, too, was panting, bent and hanging onto the banister as if it were the only thing keeping him upright. Natalie could see a spot of darkness come to life on the front of his shirt where the knife had been. Blood. It had been a closer call than Natalie even realized.

"Gabriel," she said, starting toward him. "Are you okay?"

But she was cut off by a scream and a whoosh, as the mountain lion leaped down the entire flight of stairs in one bound. Natalie ended up clutching Gabriel instead, her heart racing, as she braced herself for the grizzly sound of the cat attacking John.

But all she heard were screams coming from the doorway. The mother and daughter were huddled there, hanging on to each other, as they stared out with wide eyes. Natalie supposed that, at this point, they were unsure who exactly was the bad guy here.

There was a short shriek from the stairwell, compounded by a sigh of pain. Natalie didn't want to think about what might be happening down there.

"Shh, shush!" she hissed at the two women. "Please, stop."

The mother and daughter quieted, and Natalie strained to listen for clues about whether or not John was moving, but all she heard was silence.

A chill went down her spine.

All she heard was silence.

She shot up straight. Silence. That wasn't right.

She should have at least been hearing Jed.

She shushed everyone again and listened extra hard. Jed was no longer crying out or banging on things.

That could only mean one thing, as far as Natalie was concerned.

The man who had twice tried to kill her was roaming free in this dark hotel searching for her. And if John had found the kitchen knives, chances were very high that Jed would find them, too.

"What is it?" Gabriel whispered.

"Into the room," Natalie said, pulling on his arm. "Get back into the room."

But when she turned, she saw that the mother and daughter had backed through the doorway and were only peeking out at them through a slim opening.

"Shut it," the daughter was saying, shoving on the door.

The mom held it so that it kept bouncing back

against the force. She made eye contact with Natalie, and Natalie was sure that she was simply trying to decide if Natalie and Gabriel could be trusted. She gave her head a scared little shake, coming down on the side of uncertainty.

Natalie knew she was going to be shut out before the woman even did it.

"Don't," she said, trying to implore, but sounding too desperate. Scaring them further.

"Mom, shut it!"

The mom looked at her daughter and then back to Natalie. She bit her lip and gave that tiny headshake again.

And just as Natalie lunged for the door, Mrs. Carrington let it shut, leaving Natalie and Gabriel in darkness.

Gabriel knew that, if he got to the end of this thing alive, he had a lot of thanking to do. Thanking God but also thanking Natalie. Or maybe thanking God for bringing him Natalie. Or all of the above. That battle with John had been a very close call. If she hadn't done what she'd done, he would've been the one lying on the floor, for sure.

"No, please," Natalie moaned, leaning on the door, her palm flat against it. "Everything we need is in there."

He raised a fist to bang on the door, but Natalie stopped him.

"We don't know where he is," she whispered.

True, it seemed that Jed could be around just about

any corner. Where Gabriel wasn't imagining the mountain lion, waiting to pounce, he was imagining Jed waiting to do the same. Every shifting shadow contained another knife, another bellow of white-hot rage, another test of strength that he honestly didn't know if he could pass.

"Can we sneak into the next room?" Gabriel asked.

Natalie shook her head and gestured toward the closed door. "My key is inside."

"And my keys," Gabriel said.

She nodded. "Everything."

"So we need a new plan. We can't just stay here waiting for Jed to find us. We're sitting ducks. If he sees what happened to his brother…"

"Or if his brother wakes up…" Natalie added.

Gabriel didn't want to point out that his brother had been silent since hitting the bottom of the stairs and the cat pouncing on him. He didn't need to point it out; Natalie knew, even if she didn't want to face that she knew.

"Is there…a pantry? Closet? Anything?"

Natalie paused, and then he felt her hand clasp around his wrist again. Her hand was warm and soft, and in any other situation, it would've thrilled him every time she touched him. He would have lived for her to clasp his wrist, to tug him along. Again, he had a brief moment of indulging a thought that they were just a normal couple embarking on a normal adventure together. It was a thought that warmed him more and more every time he conjured it.

"I've got it," she said. "Follow me."

With John at the bottom of the steps, they had to traverse the long hallway to the stairs on the other end—the ones that led down into the kitchen. Natalie walked briskly, but cautiously, as if something inside her had been emboldened or renewed. Even in the dark, he could tell that she was seeing every moving shadow, hearing every creaking board. But it wasn't intimidating her. It was empowering her to move ever faster and with more confidence.

They swept through the kitchen and out the door that led to the woodpile and the back yard beyond. Gabriel thought he had been cold inside the powerless lodge, but when the wind smacked him, he realized how much colder he was about to be. He hunched his back against it and plowed forward through the snow behind Natalie.

She led him around the side of the lodge and down the slope to the lift terminal.

"I never locked it," she said, almost to herself, then threw her head back and said, "Jordan, you irresponsible genius, I'm giving you a raise." She opened the door and they both went inside. She took care to lock it behind them. "Come on."

Gabriel had never been inside a lift station before and was surprised to find how sparse it was. Mostly just a desk dominated by a control pad, and an old, worn, vinyl stool that looked out a large window at the lift that climbed the mountain.

It was really a spectacular view, forcing your eyes upward. It would be fun watching the excited skiers out here, he thought, and seeing the exuberant smiles as they came back down the mountain.

Natalie rummaged through a box under the desk and produced a pair of gloves. "Lost and found," she said, handing them to Gabriel. "People drop things from the lift all the time and never come back for them. We make a sweep about once a week during the winter months." After donning the gear, she reached into a cabinet and pulled out a blanket, letting it droop over her arm. Noting the look of wonder on Gabriel's face, she added, "Never been inside a terminal before, I'm guessing."

"Oddly, it's one place that private investigation has not taken me. And it has taken me to a lot of strange places."

"Anything as strange as what just happened in there?" she asked, nodding toward the lodge.

"Definitely not. I've been in some dangerous situations before, but nothing like this. These guys are undeterrable."

She chewed her lip, thinking, and Gabriel could see the cloud of bad memories cross over her face. He wrapped his arms around himself. "I wouldn't have thought it possible, but it somehow manages to be even colder up here."

She held out the blanket. "That's what this is for. I figured we could share it, hunker down in here, wait it out until we come up with a new plan. If we hide, he won't see us through the window. If the snow keeps up and fills in our footprints, he'll have no idea we were ever here."

"God willing," Gabriel said.

She let out a sniff of doubt as she crawled under the desk, unfolded the blanket and wrapped it around her shoulders, leaving enough for him to crawl in and join her.

"What was that?" he asked, following her lead.

"What was what?"

"That noise you just made. When I said *God willing.*"

"Oh." She paused, as if this was territory she didn't much like going into. "I just don't know how much I believe in that whole God-will-take-care-of-you business. Isn't it under God's control whether or not to let things like this happen? What did I ever do to deserve Jed Grunder? Not once, but twice."

"You don't deserve it, of course," Gabriel said softly. "And I don't know why God lets bad things happen. But you're still alive, right? That's a God thing, too."

He could feel Natalie shivering under her side of the blanket, and he wanted to scoot closer to her, to put his arm around her to help warm her up. But he suspected the shivers weren't only from the cold. He suspected that nerves were coursing through her, allowing her to feel everything that had been happening.

"I was falling for him," she blurted. "Jed. He was so nice to me, and we seemed to have things in common. He was lying to me the whole time, covering up who he really is, and I bought it, because it was the Jed I wanted him to be. The entire time I've been up on this mountain…all of the overthinking I've done on that ledge… I've been begging God to help me get over what happened, but also to understand it. Help me see how I could have been so blind. How He let me be so blind. And He never has given me any clarity. I'm just as blind as I was the day Jed left me on those stairs.

"And the thing is, I knew that I was blind. That's why I stayed up here. I figured, if God will let that happen to me, I can keep it from happening again. And I was wrong. Jed came back. Or maybe God brought Jed back, I don't know. I was blind again, and here he is again. Only this time it makes even less sense. At least the first time, I could say I was in the wrong place at the wrong time. But this…this is targeted. God is letting Jed target me. Why? What have I done? I've been minding my own business up here. Just taking care of my customers and the animals and giving up love and…"

She stopped short, pulled her knees to her chest and laid her forehead on them, burying her face against them.

"And…?" Gabriel prodded.

But she simply shook her head, refusing to answer. He was pretty sure he knew what the *and* was, though. Giving up love and vowing to be alone. Something he had also done. Something he was finding harder and harder to do the more he was near Natalie.

"When John had that knife at my chest…" Gabriel's hand automatically rose to feel the sore prickle where the knife had been pressed. He cleared his throat and started over. "When John had that knife at my chest, all I could think about was that if I died, he would come after you. So I asked God to give me strength. Somehow, I've gotten the strength to over-power each of them. And, with John, if I hadn't over-powered him, I would be dead. Was that an answered prayer? I don't know. But I think it was."

"He wouldn't have had to answer that prayer if He hadn't let this happen in the first place," Natalie said.

"Okay. I get that," Gabriel said. "But what I'm say-ing is…while my being here when this whole thing happened might have been God letting something bad happen to me, we've survived. That has to be something God let happen, too. All I know is, every time I've been in a bad situation, God is there to help me out."

"You didn't come up here for this. You came to the Hideaway to make a job decision and look what happened to you," she said bitterly.

"I met you. That happened to me, too."

She turned her head so that her ear was resting on her knees, her hair half falling over her face. Her eyes still managed to sparkle, even through all of this.

"I can't trust my gut," she said, and he knew that she meant she couldn't trust her gut about him.

"I'm not Jed Grunder."

"My brain knows that. But my heart…"

"Is scared," he finished for her. "I get that. Mine is, too. I was prepared to ask a woman to marry me. I had the ring, I was making plans, I was confident and excited. And I wanted to scope out the perfect time to do it, so I followed her for a day. And… I discovered that she was having an affair. With my best friend."

Natalie let out a little gasp. "That's terrible."

He nodded. "It took me a long time to get past it. I blamed myself for invading her privacy, which is so silly, and I knew it, but I did it. And I beat myself up for not being good enough. On top of that, I was angry at her, angry at him. Angry at everyone, really. This was supposed to be the rest of my life, and my plans, my dreams. Everything was just ripped away from me.

"I decided to uproot my entire life. I sold my house and moved. I quit taking cases and got a job in a law firm as a researcher. I've been up here trying to decide if I want to make that permanent. Become a lawyer, put away bad guys like Jed, use my skills in a different way. I felt called to come up here. And I thought that coming to a decision about my future was the reason why. But now I'm thinking I was called up here to meet you. That maybe my future is about more than my job."

"You don't know me. Not really."

"No, that's not what I meant. What I meant was I think I was supposed to meet you so I could see that I'm not ready to move on. I'm not in love with Liane anymore. But I'm not in a position to love anyone. So… I get it. My heart is scared, too. It's scared of you."

She stared at him in the dark confines of the space under the cabinet for a long time, her hair falling over one eye, her hands clasped firmly around her knees.

Curled up under the desk like two children afraid of thunder, Gabriel thought. And maybe the thunder that was scaring them was actually the roar of two hearts breaking again, their beats falling out of rhythm. At least Natalie had stopped shivering, her warmth stretching out under the blanket and warming him, too.

Finally, she chuckled, and turned her head so she was facing her knees again. She softly bounced her forehead against them.

"What's so funny?"

She shook her head as she continued to laugh, then took a deep breath and sat up straight, allowing her hands to fall away from her knees.

"It's just that I finally find the right man," she said, "and it's at exactly the wrong time. We're perfect for each other—we can both see that—and yet we would never work out."

Gabriel knew this was true—they'd just met, after all, and had a lot to work through in their lives—but there was something about hearing the words coming out of her mouth that made it even more true, and he hated it. He supposed there was a part of him that believed if neither of them said it out loud, there would still be a chance for them.

But there was no chance. Jed and Liane had taken that chance away.

And, it also turned out, Natalie was right. God couldn't help them out of this one. He'd already healed their broken hearts, and yet they were still too broken to open up again. He hated that she questioned whether or not God was with her in bad times, but it made sense to him that she did.

He sighed and let his head softly knock against the wall that propped up their backs. They'd repeatedly defeated Jed and John, so weren't they supposed to feel powerful? Shouldn't their hope about their futures be the highest they've ever been?

Maybe.

Except there was just one problem: Jed was still out there. They hadn't beaten him. Not exactly. They'd only managed to run away. So maybe running away from each other was entirely appropriate here, too.

"You're right." He rubbed his hands against his thighs, trying to warm them, get the blood circulating again. "We would never work out."

He wasn't sure he meant it. But he was sure he was meant to say it.

Chapter Eleven

Right place, wrong time. Right man, wrong woman. Right feelings, wrong histories. No matter how Natalie sliced it, it spelled out one thing clearly: she and Gabriel could never be together.

She couldn't even believe this was a conversation they were having when Jed was out there looking for them. There was no way Jed would let them off of this mountain alive. She was more certain of that than ever. Yet, at the same time, this seemed like precisely the best place and time for this conversation. In some ways, it seemed like Gabriel had been part of her life forever. But in other ways, she knew that really the man who was part of her life forever—like it or not—was Jed Grunder. Even if he wasn't chasing her around the Hideaway, he was definitely chasing her around her own head.

She'd thought she'd defeated him. Turned out, he had won all along. She'd begun to realize that, even if they were to get away from Jed, she wasn't sure how she would put the pieces back together. Especially if Cora…

Don't think that.

It seemed like there was more that needed to be said between her and Gabriel. Denying their ability to be together felt like it should have been the last word. That, after having acknowledged it, they would both be more settled. But she didn't feel more settled, and he didn't look it. And now the air between them was tense and weird, on top of the tension and weirdness that they were already dealing with. She wanted there to be a better conclusion for them, even though she knew there wasn't one. Talking about it even more would be like poking her tongue into a sore tooth. But she couldn't help herself.

"I think…" But before she could continue, a thud reverberated through the station, startling them both. Natalie pressed a hand over her mouth to keep from crying out. They stilled, and soon heard the muffle of Jed's voice.

"…in there! I'll…" *Thud, thump, thump, thud.* He was circling the station, searching for a way inside. "…wasting time…come out and face…"

She found herself pressing her shoulder closer to Gabriel's, searching for the safety of numbers. At the same time, they both scooted back as far as they could under the desk, seeking the safety of being hidden.

At this point, when her body was begging for this to just be over, Natalie needed all the strength she could get. It was too tempting to just give in. Let Jed win. Hope that it would be over as quickly and painlessly as possible, while knowing that Jed would make sure it was neither of those things.

"He followed our prints," Natalie whispered. "He knows we're in here."

Gabriel shook his head. "We can wait him out."

A gust of wind rattled through the station, finding every available crack and crevice to barge through, the tick of sleet on the windows loud and insistent, and Natalie wasn't sure how long they could wait it out here. She wasn't cold now. Adrenaline and body heat made sure of that. But eventually both of those things would wear off. And then where would they be? The storm was a third opponent for them, and in some ways more dangerous than the other two.

Not to mention, Jed was not dumb, and he was very persistent. He would keep after them—keep after his pursuit of them—until he was successful in catching them. He would find a way into the station. Natalie was sure of that. He was determined before, and he had way too much to lose now.

As if to validate her thoughts, Jed appeared at the door again, yanking so hard Natalie heard the wood of the door frame creak. This time she could hear him loud and clear.

"You killed my brother! Come out here and face me. I know you're in there!"

Natalie sucked in a breath. She supposed that a part of her knew that John's fate hadn't been good. But part of her was ignoring the possibility of how bad it had truly been. Hearing aloud that he was dead hurt her in a way she hadn't experienced before. Even if he'd been trying to kill them, she wasn't sure how she felt about having taken someone else's life. She'd only meant to save Gabriel. And it had happened so quickly, so easily. In the space of a second, a man went from alive to dead, and she was the reason. Whether the fall killed him, or the cat killed him, she was the one who set both of those things in motion.

"You won't escape, Natalie! You might as well stop putting off the inevitable! I will burn it down if that's what it takes."

"He's playing mind games with you." Gabriel seemed to sense the sliding feeling that Natalie was having. "Don't listen to him."

Thud, bang! More wrenching sounds as Jed pulled on the door. "You were so tough in the courtroom. What happened?"

"It's impossible not to listen to him."

"No, it's impossible not to *hear* him. But listening to him is another matter. You can't let him get to you. You have to stay strong, or he'll be right. You won't get away."

Jed's voice went high as he mimicked Natalie. "I had a crush on him, Your Honor. I thought he was going to ask me out. I wanted to spend time with him."

Natalie pressed her palms to her eyes. "It feels like I never will get away, no matter what. He'll always be out there. I'll always be waiting for him to find me and finish the job."

"Then we have to make sure he's not out there. The police are on their way."

"Maybe."

"We need to be positive. They *are* on their way. You can bet those two women have called them again. Now they know there are more of us up here."

"Okay, fine, the police are on their way. But what about right now? Until they get here? We can't hide in here forever. He'll get in. From the sound of things, sooner than later."

Gabriel nodded thoughtfully. "You're right. We have to go on the offensive. We had Jed trapped and unable to get to us once. We can do it again. We just need a plan."

They spoke softly, just below a whisper, the sounds of the storm masking their conversation.

"I'm tired of making plans. They don't work. I'm exhausted and you're exhausted and the only one whose plans have actually worked is Jed."

"That's not true. If his plans worked, we would already be dead. You can't think that way." He reached down and laced his fingers through hers; gave her hand a squeeze. "Natalie, regardless of what our futures look like and whether or not they can include each other, we have been brought together for a reason. We can't ignore that. We're strong together. We've beaten so much. We've stayed alive this long. We'll stay alive until they get here. I'm confident."

Natalie's mind swirled and whirled, searching for a way to make this true, the warmth of Gabriel's palm against hers emboldening her. She felt protected, surrounded, part of something bigger—greater—than herself.

The wind blew again, and she became aware of the creak of the lift line swaying under its force. It would be brutal to try and be up on the lift in weather like this. She would never run it. It would be dangerous—if you didn't fall from the bench, you would certainly struggle against the elements. You'd be frostbitten before you got to the top.

The mountain was as dangerous as it was beautiful, its ability to destroy as limitless as the sky that communed with it. Only the heartiest creatures survived the mountain on days like this.

And Natalie had survived.

She had survived.

She would continue to survive.

"You're right," she said, finally breaking contact between her hand and Gabriel's, speaking with confidence that she wasn't quite convinced she had but remained convinced enough to fake it. And after all, wasn't that really the only confidence you needed? The blanket fell off of her shoulders as she sat straighter. "I have an idea."

It was crazy. Brilliant, but crazy. But wasn't all of this crazy? Wasn't whispering about it in a dark corner beneath a desk crazy? Shouting madman outside, circling the station, yanking on the door to be let in, spouting all sorts of hate and threats…crazy, right?

God, what am I doing here? Gabriel had silently pleaded when they'd first crammed themselves under the desk. He hadn't expected an answer, and he hadn't gotten one.

Or maybe he had.

Because Natalie's idea was crazy, but it was bold and it was brave and it was all the things that she was and he fell for her all the more because of it.

Even if he knew that falling for her was a waste of his time and energy. *And don't forget a waste of your heart.*

Was it, though? His heart had been shut down to so much as a flutter since the Liane fiasco. He'd been sure he would never heal. Would never love again. This came way too close to loving. So close he almost couldn't recognize it as anything but.

He would let Natalie go. From his life, from his heart. He knew that he would. He would let her go on about her life, and he would go on about his life, and he would make his decisions and she would hide from her past and they would go their separate ways and live their separate lives, and then his life would one day require him to act bravely, and he would think of this moment. He would remember whispering under the desk. He would remember the desperation in Jed's voice and the watery fear in Natalie's bright eyes and the way her voice shook when she proposed her plan. He would remember the woman from the mountain, and it would embolden him to be better.

"The lift," she said, as if those two words explained everything. And they kind of did, but Gabriel motioned for her to keep talking, because what he thought she meant couldn't possibly be what she actually meant. It was too risky, too dangerous. "I'll go up the lift. He'll follow me. You can stop it half-way through, trap us both at the highest point. We'll stay there until the police come."

It was exactly what he'd thought she meant. Risky. Dangerous. Brilliant.

"But the power…" he said.

"The lift has its own generator. It's a safety backup."

"He'll hear it start. He'll come running."

"That's the point. I want him to follow."

"I should be the one to go," Gabriel said. "It should be me. Not you. You've been through enough."

"You've been through just as much," Natalie argued. "And, besides, he won't come after you. Not as easily as he'll come after me. If we separate, he will choose me. You'll be on the lift, and he will make a beeline to the station. I'll make him believe I'm heading up to the other lift station to call the police or hide or something. He'll follow, thinking he'll have me cornered."

"He'll follow—how?"

"He'll hop on a lift chair, too. I'm sure of it. He'll follow me up, thinking he will just catch me at the top of the mountain."

Gabriel didn't have her confidence in this scheme, but he wanted to trust her judgment.

"Can you even call the police from up there?"

She shook her head. "No phone. It's basically just a shed with a few supplies and a box with a kill switch."

"And you want to just trap him above the ground," he said. "Assuming he won't jump."

"It'll work, trust me. It doesn't look that high from here, but it is. And from the bench, you can very much tell how high it is. If he worked up the courage to jump, he would break every bone in his body when he landed. He'll be stuck, and we'll be safe."

Gabriel wasn't sure if that would work. Jed wasn't the smartest man in the world, but he wasn't dumb, either. He might catch on to a trap. He might refuse to follow, and then he and Natalie would be separated for no reason.

Or Jed might be too blind in his rage to catch on to much more than movement. Pure predator mode. He might actually fall for it.

"But he'll come after you right away. He'll catch you before you even get off the ground."

She bit her lip, then winced. "You'll have to delay him. I know what that means, and I'm sorry. You'll have to physically hold him back. It's the only way." She paused, sank into herself. "That's unreasonable of me to ask. You can say no. We'll think of another way."

"I'll do it," he said, touching her arm. "I'm not afraid for myself. Of course I'll do it. I'm afraid for you, though. It's risky."

"Doing nothing is riskier," Natalie said, and he could see her resolve in those shining green eyes. She was finished with this cat-and-mouse game and was ready to put it all to an end. "Living the rest of my life in fear of Jed is the risk I can't take. I might as well have died at the bottom of that staircase if I do nothing now."

"What if…what if you freeze up there?" Gabriel asked. "What if the police don't come for a long time and you don't make it that long? The wind will rip right through you."

Natalie swallowed. He could tell that this was the one thing she had no answer for.

"I'll hold him longer," Gabriel said, answering his own question. "I'll hold him as long as I possibly can. Let you get to the top."

"It's twelve minutes to the top," Natalie said quietly. "And that's without the wind."

"So I'll hold him for twelve minutes."

"I'll drop as soon as I safely can."

"Not a second sooner. If you break an ankle, we are as good as dead."

She nodded. "Right. I know this mountain. I know exactly where I can drop safely." She scooted forward and reached up, opening the top drawer of the desk. "There's a key ring in here. The shed is locked, and the kill switch also requires a key. And there's an ATV we might be able to get going. We haven't used any of these things this year, but the keys should still be here. Cora keeps them here because Jordan… I just need to…" She rooted around, blind, and then pulled down a set of keys, which jingled in her hand. "Thank you, Cora! And thank goodness Jordan is so forgetful. Again." She chuckled, and then her chuckles turned to deeper laughs, her chest heaving and her face scrunched up so that Gabriel might have never known the laughs turned to sobs if he hadn't seen the tears cascading down her cheeks. This was all so much, he didn't blame Natalie for the emotional release.

He reached out and pulled her to him. She remained curled into a C with her knees to her chest, her shoulders rounded, her head down. But she allowed her face to rest on his shoulder, and soon the wetness of her tears seeped through his shirt. Or maybe he just thought they did. Regardless, they were warm and full of life. And full of hurt and regret. And, yes, full of fear, too.

Finally, she sat up, away from him, and sniffed. "I'm sorry. It's just Cora…"

"I know," he said.

"If we fail…"

"I know."

"We can't fail, Gabriel."

"We won't."

She wiped her eyes and then, midswipe, froze. "Do you hear that?"

Gabriel cocked his head. "I hear nothing."

She nodded. "He's quiet."

"Do you think he went back inside?"

"I think whatever's he's doing, it's not good. He's biding his time. But I also think that means it's time for us to move."

Gabriel, unable to help himself, tucked a loose strand of her hair into her stocking cap with one gloved finger, then shed his gloves and gave them to her. "Put these over yours."

"But what about…?" But she stopped as she realized, and silently acknowledged, that Gabriel would need bare fists for what he was about to do. She nodded, took the gloves and put them on over hers. He also shed his stocking cap and placed it over hers.

"I want you to know how much I appreciate everything you've done," Natalie said, bundled up and ready to go. "I could never repay you."

"I wouldn't want you to."

"If I don't make it…if he catches up with me…"

"No," Gabriel said. "I'm not even going to let you think that way. You're getting up there. We're putting this to an end."

She gazed at him for a long while, and then nodded. She still said everything she meant to say with that gaze. He understood it all.

"Okay," she said. "I'm ready."

She stood and walked toward the door, then reached out and turned the doorknob. Ready to be the bait that would lure Jed Grunder up the mountain, and ultimately take him down.

Chapter Twelve

When the wind hit Natalie in the face, she braced herself, ready to encounter a surge of fear, but all she could muster was a sense of being fed up. She'd had enough. She wanted this to end. A feeling of resolve and acceptance of whatever may come her way.

It was the same feeling she'd had when she approached the prosecutor, Maeve Shoals, for the first time.

I want to testify, she'd said, standing in Maeve's office doorway all those years ago.

Maeve had looked up at her in shock, a pencil frozen in air over a legal pad. *You sure you want to do that? It can be brutal.*

What I'm living with is brutal. What Jed Grunder did to me was brutal. The idea of him somehow beating the system and walking free is brutal. Testifying is right. I want to feel something right for a change.

And so she did testify. She provided every piece of evidence she could think of, including the broken key that had snapped off in the lock when she fell away. She showed up in the courtroom every day, chin lifted, eyes dry, and watched as they flashed photos of the crime scene, her blood splashed on the steps, on the walls. She clenched her jaw and watched herself star in a slideshow of the ICU, her body a lacework of bandages, her face a purple-and-green patchwork of bruises, her shoulder sliced where her purse strap had been.

And after all was said and done, she stood and gave a victim statement.

Your Honor, she'd started, her voice watery and tentative, that cold blast of nerves raking over her once again. She'd cleared her throat and restarted. *Your Honor, a year ago, Jed Grunder took my purse. But he took so much more than that...*

She'd remained steadfast as she talked about him stealing her confidence, her happiness, her ability to trust and be open, her future. She'd turned and faced Jed and calmly told him that he was done taking from her, and if there was any justice in this world, he would never see the light of day again. The jury would take that from him.

And then she'd gone home, crawled into bed and cried for half a day.

The day after the verdict, she packed her things and was gone. A week later, she was an employee at the Snowed Inn Hideaway.

It was easy to be fearless when you were in a courtroom. There were protections. Barriers and lawyers and handcuffs and bailiffs with guns. Out here on the mountain, stepping into the cold wasn't quite as easy. She was alone against him. He could be waiting around any corner, and the whistling wind made him impossible to hear.

But, she reminded herself, *if you can't hear him, he can't hear you, either.*

She stepped out into the snow and hurried around to the back of the station, where the generator sat, waiting to be revved into life. Once she got it going, Gabriel could turn on the lift itself.

She and Jordan had just tested it three days prior, which now seemed like a lifetime ago. It had taken some coaxing, some fresh gasoline, and more than a few attempts, but they'd gotten it up and running. And now Natalie was eternally grateful that they'd done that minor maintenance task. She knew that it would roar into life right away.

Her fingers felt clumsy inside the double layer of gloves as she fumbled in her pocket for the generator key, but with a little digging she was finally able to grasp it. Her hands shook, the key clacking around the outside of the lock before sinking in. She knew it only took seconds, but it felt like hours of frustrating effort, and she nearly cried out when her key finally found home. It turned with a crunch of ice, but the door was crusted shut.

"No," she said, tugging with the key. The door to the control panel didn't move. "Come on, come on." She glanced over her shoulder. Fortunately, Jed was nowhere to be seen. She pulled again. "Come on. Open."

But instead, the tiny key bent. Déjà vu. Natalie sucked in a breath.

Oh, thank goodness, it's you. I have all these groceries and I can't get into my...

Surely this wasn't going to be how it ended for her a second time.

"No," she said. "Absolutely not."

She twisted the key back to starting position and pulled it out, then slid it down the frozen-over door crack, knocking out ice, and banged on the hinges with her gloved hand to break them loose, as well.

When she put the key back in, it turned much easier, and, to her relief, after the tiniest stubborn hesitation and extra tug, the door opened, revealing the control panel inside.

"Thank you," Natalie breathed. "Thank you, thank you." Gabriel claimed that God wasn't necessarily there to keep bad things from happening, but that He was there to see you through when you were walking that bad path. In the past, Natalie would have thought it was a nice sentiment, but she wouldn't have been convinced that he was right. She would have thought it was a pretty raw deal to be steadfast and faithful, only to have the world ripped out from under you. But there was comfort in the mental image of God's strong hand helping her break the crust of ice on that door, strength in knowing that she wasn't alone in this. She supposed this feeling of comfort was God's presence, and in that moment, she realized she'd felt it many times before, especially on the mountain.

God had been there with her, even when she refused to recognize Him.

Giving another glance over her shoulder, she punched the reset button and then the green start button. A part of her expected nothing to happen. But, to her relief, the engine sputtered, and then chugged, into life. After an entire day of creeping around, trying not to be heard, the running engine sounded incredibly loud. Natalie cringed, expecting Jed to appear out of nowhere, drawn to the noise like a moth to light. Instantly ready to pounce on her. End things.

But he didn't appear. And, as planned, the lift started moving—Gabriel executing his part perfectly. A chair rounded the corner, and, without a second thought, Natalie jumped on it.

Slow. Why had she never noticed before how slow the lift was? Twelve minutes in the air seemed like a short amount of time when you were catching your breath between runs and enjoying the scenery. But now it was an eternity.

The line pulled her past the station, where she saw Gabriel standing in the doorway looking tense and agitated, coiled to spring into action. They locked eyes. Natalie opened her mouth to speak but realized she didn't need to. Everything that needed to be said had been said. In some ways, this felt exactly right— Natalie being tugged away from him. Leaving him behind to tend to a fear that she didn't want to face. She didn't want to. But she had to.

In a perfect world, we may have been just right together, she thought. *But there is no such thing as a perfect world. This is the world we've been given. It's unfair and wrong and sad, but it's our reality.*

She was so riveted to Gabriel's face and the thoughts that were swirling through her mind, she almost didn't notice his mouth was moving. His arms were moving. No, he was pointing. And running. Toward her.

She couldn't hear him over the chug of the generator.

She turned to look forward and saw her worst nightmare. Jed had come from the woods opposite the lodge and was racing toward her, shoes slipping on the snow. They'd been so sure he had gone back into the lodge, they'd never even considered he might be waiting to pounce from somewhere else. He was going to get to her before Gabriel could help her.

Natalie's bench was climbing but still in reach. Too soon. He was coming at her too soon. She pulled her feet up onto the seat, but she was a second too late. Jed had closed the distance and lunged forward, hands outstretched. As he went down, one hand snagged her ankle. The force of his fall and weight of his body wrenched Natalie from her seat. She screamed and hooked her elbow through one armrest in a desperate attempt to keep from falling right on top of him.

The lift made a grinding noise as the bench temporarily stopped forward motion but then continued on, the weight of Natalie and Jed together bending the line, dragging her closer to the ground. Dragging him along with her.

"No," she huffed, kicking at Jed's hands, arms,

face. The armrest dug painfully into her elbow, causing her to slip. She was slowly inching toward letting go. "You will not..."

But Jed wasn't about to let go. His hand was like a vise around her ankle, the pain of his fingers digging into her skin as present as the metal armrest grinding against her bones. She felt like she was being stretched and would snap in half.

Somehow, she found the strength to pull her other arm up and wrap it around the armrest, as well, giving some relief to the hooked arm. But now she was fully off the seat, dangling. Panic welled inside of her. If she didn't let go soon, she would be too high off the ground to drop. But if she did drop now, she would fall right into Jed's arms.

Kick, Natalie, kick, she thought, and somehow her body got the message and began to obey. She kicked and stomped, every movement weakening her grip on the armrest. Worse, the blows seemed to do nothing to budge Jed's hand. She could hear him growling in pain and frustration, but his fingers only tightened in response.

And then she landed a blow directly onto his knuckles. He howled, and his hand slipped a few inches. Emboldened, Natalie began kicking at double speed, connecting again and again. His hand slid, slid, slid onto her shoe.

She felt her shoe loosen, and then give, and then suddenly she felt lighter as Jed fell away, her shoe hitting the snow and bouncing away. She caught a glimpse of Gabriel on the ground, pulling Jed around the waist, helping. He tumbled backward, carrying Jed with him, and the two rolled.

Her concentration broke, and her hooked arm gave way. Again, she cried out in terror, her fingers clenching and grasping for anything they could find purchase on. At first, it was only air, but at the last moment, they slid into the crack between boards on the bench seat. Once again, the bench groaned and snapped the line to a stop, but then it continued on. With Jed's weight gone, the bench lurched to a faster speed, and it felt like only moments until the ground looked small and far away. Her dangling toes grazed the tops of some of the smaller trees. She was at least twelve feet off the ground and climbing.

Seven years ago, in the wake of Jed's attack, Natalie would have never called herself strong. In fact, she would have berated herself for being the opposite. She would've blamed herself for being a victim. Cursed her poor judgment, regretted how quickly she was willing to give in and give up in the face of danger.

That Natalie would have never pulled herself back onto the bench. She would have dangled and then dropped, a broken, painful landing in the trees and weeds and packed ice and snow. But that Natalie was nowhere near as weak as she thought she was, and this Natalie understood that fact much better.

She gritted her teeth and pulled, bending her arms, her frozen fingers inside of their gloves numb and creaking. She moved one hand and then the other to the very back of the bench, her arms stretched over the wooden seat. Panting, gasping, she pulled again, inching her body up and up, until she was able to get a knee on the wood, and then a foot, and eventually her belly. She squirmed, the bench swinging and jolting, until she was sitting safely, sobs and exhaustion raking out of her in jagged, painful gasps.

That had not gone at all like she'd planned.

But she was getting closer to the top. She could see the other station ahead. It wouldn't be too long before she would be at a safe enough height to drop, and then she could run the rest of the way. Gabriel only had to hold Jed for a few more minutes, and then he could let him go. She would be far enough ahead.

She swiveled to see how Gabriel was doing.

She gasped.

She had turned just in time to see Jed hold up a knife, identical to the one John had brandished in the hallway. A knife from her own kitchen.

"Gabriel!" she shouted.

But he didn't hear her.

Jed swung the knife high over his head and plunged it downward. Gabriel reeled backward and then dropped, his hands clutching his side. Even from this distance, Natalie could see the blood materialize on the snow.

All that was on Gabriel's mind was keeping Jed busy for just a little longer. Hang in for another second, another minute, two minutes. The plan had already gone sideways. Jed had popped out from the trees on the other side of the station. They weren't expecting that. Gabriel had been ready for him to come from the lodge or the backyard or even from behind the generator. He would have been able to intercept him from any of those places. But he'd appeared from the opposite direction. Obviously waiting for them to decide to come out. When or how he'd sneaked into the woods without them seeing him, Gabriel didn't know.

All he knew was Jed had grabbed Natalie and Natalie had looked like she was falling, and Gabriel could not let that happen. He had to stop this, once and for all, no matter what it took.

He didn't feel the knife go in. Not really. He only felt his muscles betray him on one side, and a sudden inability to catch his breath. Something was wrong—very wrong—but it wasn't really sinking in what that something was.

He was so busy concentrating on his breathing, he let go of Jed. *Too soon! Too early! She hasn't had enough time!* And then in his haste to recapture Jed, he slipped on the ice and went down to one knee. He scrabbled against the snow to get back up, but one arm didn't want to work, except to clutch his side. His lungs didn't want to breathe.

And there was blood.

At first, he stared at the blood, confused. It seemed to be following him. And it seemed to be fresh. And it seemed to be growing. He didn't think that he'd gotten that many hits in on Jed, and he was sure Jed hadn't gotten that many punches in on him; how could either one of them be bleeding this much?

It only began to dimly dawn on him that the blood

could possibly be coming from his side. And that the weakness and inability to breathe could somehow to be tied to it. He was suddenly aware of a coldness against his skin, a bit of a prickle. He felt around, trying to figure out exactly what he found there. Something hard and cold and now—*oh, yeah, now*—the prickle was turning to pain. And the weakness was turning to gray.

Did he...stab me? Is this a knife? Surely not. I would know if I got stabbed, right? I would be... I would be dead. He had a jolt of realization then, but even that jolt was dulled. He just didn't seem to have the energy to be afraid. He watched as Jed— his killer—raced away from him. Raced toward a lift bench, limping and grunting and cradling one hand in the other, as if it were broken.

Farther up the lift was a small figure—Natalie, swinging on a bench, but turned around so she was looking right at him. He could feel the figure's stare more than see it from this far away. *Natalie.* The name came to him weakly—his confusion was worsening—and he tumbled it around in his head like freshly drying linen. *Natalie, Natalie, Natalie...*

"Gabriel!" the figure yelled. He heard it as clearly as if it were right next to his ear, rather than a football field away. The sound nudged him into reality.

"Natalie!" he'd yelled. He knew he had. But there was no air behind it. No volume. And why was there a gurgling feeling every time he tried to breathe?

He had a task to do. He was dimly aware of that. But the gray was starting to really press into his temples now, making it hard to think. He stared at the figure—at Natalie—and at Jed as he trundled up the lift behind her. The task had something to do with this lift. Something to do with Natalie and Jed.

Something to do with the lift.

He turned, aiming himself back at the lift station, going on instinct. He wasn't sure what he was supposed to do, but he was sure that clues would be located inside that station, and he would remember his task once he got inside. Time was running out.

He felt cold. Not cold from standing outside in the storm in a sweater and pair of jeans. Not cold from having given Natalie his hat and gloves. Cold that came from the inside first. Cold from the loss of blood that should be heating his veins. He took a step forward, wobbled and took another. A third step, and he fell, snow pressing into his nose and mouth. Now he really couldn't breathe, and every sputter felt like it took a million pounds of pressure to get out.

"Gabriel!" The sound was farther away now, but he could still hear the desperation. He lay in the snow, struck with how beautiful the deep red of blood was against the stark white of the snow. *I was here for the beauty*, he thought. *I was here to make a decision. A big one. But something happened. I made a different decision. It wasn't the right one.*

Liane flashed into his mind. She was strikingly beautiful. Way out of his league. He'd often wondered why she chose him out of all the men she could have had. He wasn't entirely shocked to discover that she'd chosen someone else in the end. He was hurt. Love for someone didn't just disappear. It faded away in painful little rips and tears. *You don't just fall out of love in an instant*, he thought. *But you sure can fall in love in that amount of time, can't you?*

Liane's face morphed. It was Natalie standing there, just out of reach. She, too, had chosen someone else over Gabriel. She'd chosen Jed. She'd chosen fear and hiding. And the pain of enduring that choice was far greater than the pain of losing Liane had ever been. Because it was just so right between them, and if he was being honest with himself, it was never this right with Liane.

You have to help me, the Natalie in his mind said. Was this a dream? Had he fallen asleep?

He blinked away a snowflake that had watered his vision. "What? Help you do what?" To anyone else, he would have looked like he was talking to himself or to no one at all. But mind-Natalie heard him loud and clear.

He's almost to the top, she said.

"Who is?" When had he fallen asleep, exactly? He was awfully cold. He must have left a window open. He needed to wake up and close the window.

You have to stop the lift. Gabriel. Stop the lift.

A surge of strength coursed through him, and for a brief second, he was right back in reality. He wasn't sleeping, and Liane had not come to him in a dream. Neither had Natalie. She was the person high on the lift who had turned around and was shouting his name in the blizzard, and his job was to stop the lift as soon as she jumped off of it. Trap Jed Grunder at the highest point.

He pushed himself out of the snow, a piercing pain in his side stealing his breath. He coughed, every hack bringing more and brighter spots of pain. He was wheezing. Or maybe more like whining. He didn't feel himself doing it, but he could clearly hear it. A high-pitched, relentless, undulating whine.

Somehow, he found the strength to push himself to his knees, and then his feet. He watched as Natalie dropped to the ground, arms wheeling, and landed in a heap in the snow. He took a step toward her but knew there was no way he would get up the mountain to where she was. His breath was coming in thick, wet gulps now. He would be doing good to just finish the task at hand. Whatever it was.

Still, she'd fallen from a long way. *She could be hurt. She could need me.*

"Natalie," he croaked.

But she didn't hear him. She didn't move at all.

Chapter Thirteen

She was thinking of bailing too early. She knew it was too early. But Jed was closer than she wanted him to be, and Gabriel was floundering on the snow down below, pinkening the white in sweeps and circles. He looked disoriented.

He looked like someone who was dying.

Natalie was shocked by the gut punch of grief she felt at the thought of Gabriel dying. The loss was palpable. After this was over, they'd planned to go their separate ways. So why was she so panicked at the thought of surviving this without him?

Because you know that chances are you won't *survive without him. You need him just as much as he needs you. Maybe more.*

The plan had been for Gabriel to stop the lift as soon as Natalie jumped and Jed was too high to jump. But Gabriel had fallen facedown in the snow. And now it was all on her to finish the job. She wanted to be strong enough to do it alone, but she wasn't entirely convinced she was actually that strong. The past would argue that she wasn't.

But that's not true, a little voice in the back of her mind said. *You survived before. You will survive again.*

And you are anything but alone.

Again, she felt washed over by the feeling of God's presence, a hand reaching toward her, if only she would take it. She had to take it. She was in love with Gabriel, and there was no way she was going to let him die.

"God," she said aloud. "I need to lean on you right now. Please be my strength." These were the same words she'd thought as she'd walked into the courtroom on the day Jed was found guilty. Only now it wasn't just a spiritual insurance policy. Now, she believed God was listening.

She remembered that the lift terminal she was headed to wasn't just a good place to hide and wait for the police; there was an emergency shutoff in there. If Gabriel couldn't get to the controls, she could. She wasn't too far away, which was good, because her one shoeless foot was already going numb. But the shed was locked, and she wasn't sure which key opened it. Time was of the essence, not just because of Jed, but because she wanted to get on the ATV and get back down to where Gabriel was.

Don't die, don't die, don't die, she thought, as she scooted closer to the edge of the bench. Treetops were still below her feet. It was too high. But she glanced backward and saw Gabriel standing, wavering in the wind, looking lost and frightened. He wasn't going to last much longer. She had to make a move.

"Three, two, one," she counted, launching herself from the seat on *one*. Soon she was falling and falling, the cold air biting her skin on the way down. She fell straight, only bending her knees and tucking into a roll at the very last minute.

There's something magical about how snow always looks like fluff and pillows and clouds and softness—even if you know that it's not the fluffy, soft place it looks, part of you still expects it to be. She supposed she had anticipated the landing would absorb the impact from the fall. And, fortunately, she landed in a drift that was deep enough to keep her from breaking every bone in her body. But still the touchdown stung, jolting her to her core, causing her teeth to clack together, and knocking the wind out of her. She rolled, willing her body to *breathe, breathe, just take in one breath*, but it didn't want to obey. When it finally did, she was on her stomach, and she managed to inhale a mouthful of snow that choked and froze her. She coughed and sputtered, all the while assessing whether or not anything else seemed broken.

Somehow—and she didn't understand how this could even be possible—nothing was. She took a moment to fill her lungs a few times, and then rolled to her hands and knees.

Don't look back, she told herself. *Whatever you do, only look forward*. Seeing how close Jed was getting, how weak Gabriel was becoming, wouldn't help her in any way. She knew this, yet it was almost impossible to just keep looking in front of her. She wanted to know. Even if knowing would terrify or destroy her.

She popped up to her feet, feeling the ground beneath her. This mountain was her friend. Her safety. She'd always felt protected here, although by whom she couldn't quite say. By anonymity? By isolation?

This mountain is mine, and how dare Jed Grunder barge into my space!

Suddenly, she felt angry. For the first time. It had always been about justice, about fear, about regret and guilt and self-condemnation. She'd never allowed herself to truly just be mad. Until now.

She clenched her jaw and plugged forward through the snow, up and up those last few feet to the tiny lift station. She felt steadier than she had before. More confident. She could do this. There was absolutely no reason that she couldn't.

The shed door was padlocked. She fished around in her pocket until she came up with the key ring again. On a normal day, she would likely be able to identify the right one just by looking at them. But everything looked different when you were running for your life. Everything was murky and confusing.

She chose a key, inserted it and turned. Wrong one. She tried another. Wrong. She felt her pulse in the base of her throat. A third key. Still not the right one. Had she already tried that one before? She thought she hadn't, but maybe she had. Wrong, wrong, wrong. Her breath started coming in short, shallow pulls, and her hands started shaking again. *Don't look back, do not look back...*

She dropped the key ring. It disappeared into the snow, burrowing its own little hole and hiding inside.

"No," she said, and in her horror, she did look back. In the matter of a couple minutes, Jed would be getting close enough to jump safely. She couldn't even see Gabriel anymore.

"No!" she yelled. "I can't... Not this way!" She dropped to her knees and began wildly scooping at the snow with her hands, barely even aware of the cold melting through her gloves, digging into her fingers.

Who cares about cold fingers when Gabriel could be down there already gone?

She heard the faint *clink* of metal bumping against metal and sifted through the snow more carefully, leaning forward until her hands were on the keys. She sprang back to her feet and blindly jammed a key into the lock. It turned.

She wrestled the lock off the door and tossed it to the side and burst into the shed. It was dusty, and a spider had busily webbed the little control box, making it look as if it had been longer than it had been since anyone was last up here. Natalie brushed away the web and fumbled through her keys again. This time she easily found the right one, but just as she was preparing to stick it into the lock, she became aware of a sound that had been chipping away at the back of her mind for some time now. A high, persistent screech.

Police sirens.

The police were on their way.

And from the way the sirens swooped and looped over each other, there were a number of them. Plodding through the storm, putting their own lives at risk to save hers. They weren't super close, but they were audible over the wind, which made them close enough.

Relief so powerful it felt like giddiness bubbled and frothed in her chest, until she let it out in a triumphant laugh that hurt her throat.

It was going to work. The plan was going to work. She just had to hit the kill switch and Jed would be stuck. He wouldn't have enough time to figure out a plan to get down. He would still be swinging on the line when the police arrived. She could get off the mountain. She could live her life.

Whatever that would look like. A distant part of her understood that it would look very different from the past six years. Turned out hiding didn't work. The bad guys could still find you. There was no place to hide from your memories, anyway.

She turned back to the control box, inserted the key and turned it. Nothing happened.

"What?" she said, twisting the key off and on again. "It's not…? This isn't possible." She began urgently pressing the emergency stop button, just in case it was only the light that wasn't working. But the hum of the lift continued. "This can't be happening." She used her fist to pound the side of the box, took her key out to try another, pushed all of the buttons over and over. Anything to just get the lift to stop moving.

Desperate, she went to the shed door, now completely unable to stop herself from looking back. Time warped and distorted around her; this had all seemed to happen in slow motion, but Jed was coming up the mountain quickly. She stood and watched, dumbfounded. She'd come so far, only to lose this close to the end. It was unfair. It was as if she was meant to be killed by Jed Grunder and maybe should have just died seven years ago to make it easier on everyone.

No, Natalie, she told herself. *You can't be thinking like that. You can't give up. You can hide again.*

But she was tired of hiding. She was tired of fighting. She just wanted to be.

She was about to talk herself into surrender when she saw movement at the bottom of the mountain. Gabriel was still alive! He was moving. And now she could see the trail of dirty snow where he'd wallowed and dragged himself to the station door.

He pulled himself to standing, turned, and gave her a wave.

If he was going to give up on himself, fine. But Gabriel could not give up on Natalie. Before he let himself be defeated, he needed to make sure she was okay. He needed to finish his part of the plan. He owed her that, at least.

His side ached. His lungs felt like deflated balloons. His lips, at first tingling, were now numb. So were his fingers. And he'd started to lose feeling in his feet. There was a lot of him spilled out onto the snow. It hardly seemed possible that he could still be alive. Still be upright.

But he wouldn't be upright without the help of this doorframe, and somehow, he had to cross through the threshold and leave it. Somehow, he had to traverse to the other side of the room. The lights glared at him. He knew which button to push. He just didn't know how he would ever get there.

Natalie was watching. He'd waved at her and she'd waved back. She'd gestured toward the lift. Message received: *Stop Jed now.*

His head swam as he turned away from her and back toward the door. There was that whine again. It was getting louder. Did death come with a squeal? He'd never heard anything like that, but he supposed anything was possible.

No. Wait.

He paused, leaned his head on the doorframe, closed his eyes, concentrated. This was a sound he recognized. He'd heard it before; he just had to place it. Why was it so hard to think?

Siren. It was a siren. He thought he remembered they'd called the police, but that seemed like years ago. Had they really only been at this a few hours?

"Ambulance," he croaked, his breath coming out in smoky little puffs against the wood. "Please let there be an ambulance. I need…" He didn't have the air to finish the rest of the sentence.

You need to stop the lift, is what you need, an annoying voice in the back of his head insisted. *You need to stop Jed before he gets to Natalie.*

"Right," he said aloud, as if the voice had come from a person in the room.

He lurched through the doorway like a drunken man and aimed his body toward the desk where they'd hidden before. Five steps, tops. He could do this.

Only his legs didn't agree. They kept wanting to buckle under him, and he kept having to use furniture and equipment to stay upright. It felt a little like surfing, but instead of staying on top of water, he was trying to stay on top of his feet.

Finally, he reached the control panel, and practically collapsed on top of it. A wave of nausea had overtaken him. He felt as if he was going to be sick at any moment.

Then be sick. But first...the switch. Just push that little button right there. It's red. It's blinking. You can do this. Push, Gabriel, push.

"Yes," he said, unaware that words were coming out of his mouth. "Push the button. Exactly."

He could see Natalie through the station window. Could feel her expectation radiating down the mountain.

"I love…" The gray swarmed his head, a buzzing cloud of angry insects stealing his breath and his legs and his life. "I love…"

He could feel himself going.

He leaned forward with everything he had, so that he was practically lying across the control panel. He pressed his whole palm against the kill switch.

And pushed it as he slid to the ground, everything going black, his thoughts finally quiet.

Chapter Fourteen

There was a loud squeak that Natalie knew deep in her bones. Then the sound of motors revving down. And, finally, the grinding noise of the bench right above her swinging empty in the wind.

And then the sounds of Jed yelling.

It had worked. Gabriel had stopped the lift. Jed was stuck at the top. The sirens were coming. She was free.

She felt weak with relief and an intense desire to either high-five Gabriel or wrap him in the biggest hug in the world. For a brief moment, she stood still, unsure what to do or where to go first. Part of her wanted to just sit down and collect herself for a moment.

Go to him.

The sentence wasn't so much heard as a voice but more heard as a knowledge. Gabriel needed her. She needed to get to him. If he was savable, she needed to do the saving.

She went back into the shed where there was an ATV. But she'd had her fill of keys and fiddling. She wanted to get down the mountain fast, and she knew just how to do it.

Behind the ATV was a pile of random old skis, boots, and poles. She wasn't even sure how long they'd been there. Nobody had used them in years. Many times, she'd threatened to pitch it all in the trash but had never actually gotten around to it.

And now she was glad.

There was no faster way down for her than on skis.

She held the boots upside down and clapped them together, just in case any critters had decided to call them home, and then shucked off her remaining shoe and stuffed her feet into the boots. She carried the skis outside and let her body take over, clicking the boots into their bindings and wrapping the wrist straps of the poles around her wrists. She was hardly the best skier in the world, but she could hold her own. And she sure as the world could get down this mountain to help Gabriel.

Jed yelled in the background. He said vile things. He threatened. He cursed. He thrashed in the bench so that it seemed as if the entire line would come down.

And Natalie ignored it all. She was in her element. She had a mission. Jed was nothing to her. Not anymore.

She made her way to the top of the slope and readied herself. She could see the falling snow take on an alternating red-and-blue tinge. The police were so close now.

She pointed her skis down the slope and leaned forward, pushing her weight over them, then tucked the poles under her arms as she got moving. Quickly, she built speed, and she did nothing to slow herself. She felt like she was flying. Flying by Jed. Flying away from her past. She didn't even mind the cold wind on her cheeks or the way it ripped tears from her eyes. Flying was the best feeling in the world.

Her legs, earlier weak with fatigue, felt alive, two springs absorbing the undulation of the land. She could have kept going until she reached the bottom of the mountain. Until she reached the valley. Until she reached Colorado, Texas, the ocean. Just fly and fly and fly until she became part of the wind itself. Part of the air that Gabriel breathed.

But she couldn't keep flying. She had to keep Gabriel here on earth.

She stopped herself right outside the lift station and shed the skis quickly. She dropped the poles as she ran, clumsy in ski boots, through drifted snow and pink snow and bright red snow and into the station.

Gabriel lay on the floor, his face pale, lips blue, a growing puddle of blood beneath him.

So much blood.

"Gabriel!" She went to him, fell to her knees beside him, put her hands on his face. He felt cool, but not cold, and she could have sworn his eyes fluttered when she touched him. "Gabriel. Stay with me. The police are here. Just a few more minutes."

She searched for the source of the blood and found it, a tear in his shirt on the side, just below the ribs. He'd pulled out the knife. She could see it discarded on the floor near the door.

Without thinking, she pressed her hand against the wound, clamped it down hard. He cringed, his eyes opening fully then, but they were faraway, looking past her.

"Gabriel," she said again. "We've got to stop the bleeding, okay? We've got to…" She looked around wildly, and her eyes landed on the blanket they'd only recently been huddled under together. She snagged a corner of the blanket, balled it and held it to his side. "Just hang in there, okay? You've got to stay with me. You've got to…" To her surprise, her voice broke, and she couldn't continue.

Gabriel's eyes opened again, but this time they were present. He looked right at her. "Natalie," he said, his voice barely above a whisper. "You're here."

"I'm here. You're going to be okay."

"Jed…"

"He's trapped. Just like our plan. It's over, Gabriel. We got away. You're a hero."

His eyes slipped closed in a very slow blink, but he was still there. He was still alive. "Natalie…"

"It's okay," she said, longing to cradle his head or caress his face, be tender with him to let him know that she cared. But she had to keep pressing the wound. "It's going to be fine. He's going to be arrested, and you're going to…" She hesitated, unsure how to finish the sentence. The word *live* had been on the tip of her tongue, but to say it would be to acknowledge there was a possibility that he might not. She didn't want to acknowledge that possibility, to him, or even to herself. Not out loud. That would be like courting it. Too much.

But also there was the slight problem that she couldn't even really promise that he was going to get help. Help was on the way, but it had taken so long to get here. How would they possibly get back down the mountain and to a hospital in time to save him?

Be positive, Natalie. Trust in God, she told herself.

All I know is, every time I've been in a bad situation, God is there to help me out.

"You're going to be so proud, Gabriel," she said. "You saved us, and you saved Cora, and you're probably going to get a parade. What do you think, huh? Do you like parades?"

A smile spread across his face. Slow, but real. So real, Natalie feared that he might be slipping away, and this was the smile of a man at peace.

"Natalie," he said for a third time. "I love…"

He didn't finish. His eyes closed again, and his face went slack. His entire body seemed to relax, and only then did Natalie realize, when his hand fell away, that he had been gripping her wrist.

"No," she said, pressing harder into his side, because that was all she knew to do. "No! Gabriel! Don't you dare! Gabriel!"

The red-and-blue lights that had been bouncing off of the snow now rippled through the lift station, reflecting off of the control panel, Natalie's skin, the walls.

"Help!" she screamed as loud as she could. "We're in here! He's dying! Help us!"

Chapter Fifteen

Lying in his hospital bed, Gabriel wasn't sure what was real and what was memory. It all seemed surreal to him now. Impossible that he'd actually gone through any of it.

There was a man. No, two men. They'd attacked Cora. They'd been after Natalie.

Natalie. She was real, and he remembered every detail about her.

Beautiful owner of the Snowed Inn Hideaway, with her piercing green eyes and her wild, dark hair. She didn't smile easily, but when she did, it lit up the entire world. She bit her lip when she was thinking. She licked her lips when she was nervous. She was bold. Strong. Willing to do whatever it took to save herself. Save her friend. Save him.

She was hard on herself. He remembered that about her, too.

The door opened, and in walked his sister, Grace.

"You're awake. Finally. I brought you some doughnuts." She set a pink box on the table next to the bed, alongside the breakfast he hadn't touched. "Seriously, Gabe, you have to start eating if you ever want to get out of here."

You try working up an appetite after having a knife stuck in your gut, he wanted to say, but he knew that wasn't the problem. He wasn't eating because he wasn't hungry. And he wasn't hungry because…well, because life just didn't seem as robust as it should be. There was something missing, and he knew exactly what that something was.

He picked up a doughnut and took a small taste. Too sweet. He put it back. Grace sat next to him, leaned over to study the doughnuts, snagged one, and took a huge bite.

"So, law school, huh?" She reached into her bag and pulled out a familiar legal pad. She waved it in the air. "Looks like it won the pros list."

"Where did you get that?"

"The lady who owns the hotel gave it to me."

He scooted upright, wincing against the pull of the stitches in his side. He fought against the urge to cough, knowing that coughing only led to more coughing, which led to being unable to breathe, which led to feeling like he was going to suffocate, which led to wishing he would just to get this over with. "Natalie? You saw her?"

She nodded. "Last night. While you were asleep. She gave me this, too." She reached back into her bag and pulled out his laptop. Weird. He'd totally forgotten he'd left these things in his room at the Hideaway.

"And some other stuff that I took to my car. Suitcase, keys, that kind of thing."

"Why didn't you wake me?"

Grace shrugged, defensive. "I didn't know I was supposed to. It's not like it was important. It's just a few things you left in a hotel room."

"It's not up to you to decide what's important," Gabriel snapped.

Grace looked stung. "Sorry. I didn't know. She probably just brought it here to butter you up, anyway. Avoid a lawsuit. You are going to sue, right? I mean, since you're going to be a lawyer and all."

"No, of course I'm not going to sue," he said, taking the computer and legal pad from Grace. Then, realizing he was taking out his frustrations on Grace, who definitely didn't deserve it and was only standing in until their parents, who'd been wintering in Florida, could get to the hospital, he softened. "She didn't mean for any of that to happen. She was an innocent victim, too. And she saved my life. At least that's what I've been told."

The doctors had told Gabriel about how Natalie had stanched the stab wound, how she'd cried out for help, how when the EMTs got there, she refused to leave his side, had insisted on riding in the same ambulance. Gabriel had hazy memories of the feeling of a warm presence next to him as they slowly made their way down the mountain. A soft voice asking questions, whispering reassurances. Holding his hand. Praying. He remembered not wanting the feeling to end. But it had. And when he awoke in his hospital bed, she was not there. Gone.

Or at least that was what he had thought.

But she'd been there at least once. She'd checked on him, brought his belongings. Surely she wasn't just doing it to ensure that he wouldn't sue. Surely she had brought some of that warm hope with her.

Maybe she had even wanted to just…see him.

Maybe he was being optimistic.

"Oh." Grace swallowed her bite of doughnut, then pressed her hand to her mouth, her eyes crinkling with a smile that she was covering. "Oh. I see. You like her."

"It's not like that," he said. But he heard the weakness in his protest. He wasn't even convincing to himself.

"Yes, you do. You fell for the lodge lady." She waved what was left of her doughnut around in the air as she looked up at the ceiling, thinking. "She *was* really pretty. She had this sort of…untamed mountain look about her."

Gabriel laughed. "Untamed?"

Grace shrugged. "It's not an insult. I wish I looked like that. Natural beauty. Does she know? Does she feel the same?"

It was Gabriel's turn to shrug. He pulled little pieces of ripped paper off of the top of the pad. "It doesn't matter."

"Why? Of course it matters."

"Because we can't be together. We've been through too much. Trusting is hard."

Grace rolled her eyes dramatically. "Oh, give me a break, Gabriel. You've been stabbed in the side, and you think falling for a beautiful woman who obviously cares about you is the hard thing?"

"You don't understand, Grace." But he was wondering if maybe she did. Maybe she understood better than he did. He tossed the legal pad to the side, the pages riffling open. "I can't think about all that right now. I've got to get back to work."

"So...no law school."

"Stay the path, not the passion," he said. "It makes sense. I have a job. I'm good at it. I don't have to love it."

"Well, now you just sound like you're scared of life. Do you really want to go back to chasing bad guys? I mean, didn't you get enough of that up on the mountain?"

He didn't have an answer for her. She was just asking too many hard questions.

"I'm pretty tired, Grace. Thanks for the doughnuts. I'll eat one later." He allowed himself to sink down in his bed. He needed to be alone. He needed to think.

"Okay," she said around the final bite of her own doughnut. She stood, leaned over and kissed him on the forehead. "You're a terrible liar, by the way. And I know you won't eat the strawberry shortbread crumble. Your loss. It tastes like a Pop-Tart, and it's all mine." She plucked a fresh doughnut out of the box and crossed the room. "Get some sleep, brother. Mom and Dad will be here in about four hours, and if you think *I'm* not buying your fibs, just wait until you try to float them past Mom."

Gabriel couldn't help chuckling. She was totally right. Their mother would sense that he was holding back the minute she walked in the room. Still, he couldn't wait to see her.

Grace left, her shoes squeaking along the clean hospital tile, and Gabriel turned onto his good side, finding himself facing the legal pad that was pushed up against the bed rail, its pages splayed.

Pro: Help get dangerous criminals off the streets.

More like off the mountains, he thought.

Con: No freedom to come to the mountain.

He sank into his pillow, pondering. Grace was right; he'd had enough chasing bad guys to last a lifetime. He just found that the decision wasn't so much about his job move anymore. It wasn't the most pressing problem in his life. The most pressing problem was that he hadn't allowed himself to move on after Liane. He'd never accepted the hurt, and as a result, it had become part of him.

He noticed some writing a few pages toward the back of the pad. He tilted his head. He didn't remember writing anything back there. And the handwriting didn't even look like his. He picked up the pad and leafed through until he found the page. When he realized who had written it, he sat straight up, the stitches in his side screaming at him, but he ignored them.

Natalie.

Dear Gabriel,

I've checked on you a few times, and you're always asleep. You look so peaceful, I can't bear to wake you. I hope you're recovering well.

I know you must be wondering about Cora, so I wanted to let you know that she's alive. She was barely hanging on when they finally got up to her room, but they kept her breathing and got her down the mountain. She's just down the hall, and today she woke up. She doesn't remember a thing about what happened. They'll keep her a while longer, and then they'll let her go home.

I think that must be a God thing, her not remembering anything. He spared her, just like you said. He was there when the bad thing happened, and He's still there with her, shielding her from the worst memories.

I wish He had shielded me of the same, but if He's working overtime on the two of you, I understand and I won't complain. He's got a lot on His plate. And He was there for me when I needed him most, anyway.

I also wanted to let you know that our plan worked. The police had Jed trapped from both sides when he came down from the lift. He's back in prison, where he belongs, and will have another trial ahead. I've decided that I'll give my statement but stay away from the trial. I'm ready to put Jed Grunder totally behind me.

Surprisingly, John is not dead, either. The big cat must not have messed with him after all. I haven't really asked about scratches or bites. He's alive, and that's all I really needed to know. I didn't want to have killing him on my conscience if I could avoid it. He did have a few broken bones, and a doozy of a concussion, by the way, and is likely having plenty of headaches in jail, where he is also waiting for his trial. That part, I don't mind so much.

You never asked me what I thought you should do about this pros-and-cons list, and I totally invaded your privacy when I read it (I'm sorry about that, but not too sorry, because it helped me feel like I got to know you a little better), but I'm going to tell you anyway. Here it is, my super helpful advice:

You should do what makes you happy.

That sounds trite, I know. Really simplistic. And life is rarely, if ever, that simple. But you know how you felt when you were on the ledge, and you saw Henrietta flying around? That's what I want you to feel all the time. That's what you deserve to feel. You're so giving and so kind and so…everything good, you should have all the eagle flights. Always.

When I was skiing down the mountain to get to you, I felt like that eagle. I felt like I could conquer anything, or at least whoosh past it, untouchable. Jed was literally right over my head, and I wasn't worried. He was meaningless. I was the eagle. I was Henrietta. It was beautiful.

So...what makes you feel like you're flying? That's what you should do.

I can't thank you enough for your bravery at the Snowed Inn Hideaway. It goes without saying that we always have a room for you, although we wouldn't blame you one bit if you never wanted to walk through our doors again. After we reopen, of course. I'm not so sure if I want to walk through those doors again, either, so the Hideaway is taking a little hiatus. We've got healing to do.

And a lot of overthinking, probably.

Take care of yourself, Mr. Neesom from room 204.

Natalie

PS: The mountain lion and I have come to an understanding. He has promised to leave my friends alone, and I promised to leave him the occasional steak when I come back. His name is Brad. He's not a bad guy.

The last line made Gabriel laugh out loud, his heart feeling like it might burst with happiness that she reached out to him. He traced her name with his finger, then read the note again. And again. And again.

So...what makes you feel like you're flying? That's what you should do.

He fell asleep cradling the pad to his chest, those words echoing in his mind.

Chapter Sixteen

Natalie stepped into the Hideaway and held the door for Cora.

"Oh," Cora said when she entered and saw Ruth's bookcase lying on its side in the office doorway, its books scattered everywhere.

"Yeah," Natalie said. "I haven't had a chance to clean that up yet."

Not exactly true. She'd had the chance, she supposed, but she hadn't had the courage. Or the drive. Something like that. She hadn't been ready to face what had happened up at the Hideaway that day. She hadn't wanted to relive hurriedly trapping Jed in the office, or the Carringtons, who'd trusted him enough to try to free him but didn't trust Natalie and Gabriel enough to let them inside the safety of Gabriel's own room. Natalie tried not to be bitter about it, but that wasn't always easy, especially after she got a letter from the Carringtons' lawyer, demanding compensation for their pain and suffering.

But she also supposed she hadn't been ready to be back in the Hideaway without Gabriel, and that was the real problem.

For the month since being hunted at the Hideaway, Natalie had been staying at her mother's house in Casper, silently rattling around, wondering how she was ever going to get back to some semblance of normal, and, of course, thinking about Gabriel. Wondering how he was getting along.

Maybe you should go back up there, her mother finally suggested, and Natalie was almost shocked to find that the idea no longer scared her. She'd called Cora, and here they were, standing in the foyer, staring at a whole lot of work to be done.

Cora picked her way behind the desk, collecting books as she walked and setting them on the counter. She bent to examine the bookcase.

"Is there much damage?"

"If there is, Ruth wouldn't be mad about it," Natalie said.

Cora chuckled, pushing her finger into a gouge. "True. She probably would have shown this dent to every person who walked in here so she could tell the story. She would have been proud of you, Natalie. You know she was all about self-protection."

Ruth was fearless. She kept a shotgun behind the counter and encouraged Natalie to do the same. Now, Natalie wasn't sure if she was regretful or relieved that she'd never done it. Would she have been able to stop the whole thing in its tracks a month ago, or would Jed have gotten hold of it and ended her and Gabriel quickly?

Natalie didn't want to tell the story. She didn't want to think about it.

Cora straightened and peered into the office. "Oh," she said again.

"A lot of work to be done," Natalie agreed. She still hadn't left her spot in front of the door. *Come on, Natalie, it's one foot in front of the other. Start moving.*

"We've got time."

"I've hired a couple of housekeepers," Natalie said, finally finding the will to move her feet. She leaned on the counter across from Cora.

Cora stiffened, her eyebrows creasing. "What do you mean, a couple of housekeepers?"

"Their names are Cambria and Heidy. They'll be here this afternoon to get started."

"Oh, you mean to clean up this mess," Cora said, gesturing toward the office. "Two of them, though? Seems like a lot for one little job."

"No, they're permanent."

There was a beat of silence, during which Natalie started to worry that she was being cruel to poor, loyal Cora.

"You think I need help? It was just a bump on the noggin, Natalie. I'm fine. I can certainly push a broom."

"First of all, it was way more than a bump on the noggin, Cora, and you know it. You could have died. You almost did."

Cora waved her off. "Don't make it sound worse than it was."

"Secondly," Natalie said over her, "they're not here to help you. They're here to replace you."

"Come again? Did you say replace me? Surely you didn't say that. No offense, but I've been here longer than you have." Cora's face had begun to redden. Natalie had seen Cora frustrated plenty of times, but never actually angry.

"That's why I think you should be my co-owner," Natalie said. She reached into her bag, which she had slung over her shoulder, and produced a sheaf of papers. "I've been working on this with my lawyer. *Our* lawyer."

Cora stared, stunned, at the papers for a few seconds before reaching out to take them. "Are you serious?"

"Very. I'm sorry for pulling your leg a minute ago."

Cora was too busy being in shock to be mad. She scanned the documents, turning the pages quickly. "You really want this?"

Natalie reached across the desk and placed her hand on Cora's arm. "I was actually thinking about it before any of this happened. It's long overdue. I should have done it when Ruth died. And then when you were attacked…well, I was afraid that I'd waited too long, and it was too late. I told myself that if you made it, I wouldn't hesitate another second. You are my partner here. You don't work for me. You never did. We work together. And I want to make that official."

Cora let the papers drift to the desk and wiped one eye with a finger. "Oh, Nat. You have no idea what this means to me."

"You have no idea what *you* mean to *me*."

"Come over here," Cora said. "I need to hug you."

Natalie picked her way around the desk, nearly falling into Cora, eliciting laughs from both of them, but as soon as she was grabbable, Cora pulled her in for a hug. "Thank you."

"Thank you," Natalie said.

When they finished hugging, Cora stepped back. "Does this mean you intend to spend some time away from the Hideaway?"

"No. Why would I?"

"I know you well enough to know you've been brooding, Natalie Marlowe. If I didn't know better, I would think it was a broken heart. Is there someone that you need to tell me about?"

"Absolutely not." Natalie could feel herself flush and tried to make up for it by bending to pick up the pieces of a broken coffee mug. She stacked them on the counter.

"So there definitely is. Who is it?" She stopped Natalie from bending down for more trash. "Who is it?" she repeated.

Natalie thought about denying again but realized she would never be able to keep it from Cora, and Cora would never give up on asking. "Gabriel Neesom."

Cora drew in a breath. "Superman?" She'd been calling him that ever since Natalie told her the story of everything that happened that fateful day at the Hideaway. Cora had even taken him flowers in the hospital. She laid a palm against her chest, swooning.

"I approve! Oh, my goodness, you fell in love while saving each other. It's like a movie."

"It's like totally ridiculous. Just because I have silly feelings for someone doesn't mean he has feelings for me. Nobody said anything about love."

"But he does."

"What do you mean, he does?"

"He does have feelings for you. When I went to visit him, he must have asked about you twenty times. It was obvious."

Gabriel asked about her? Natalie wasn't sure why this surprised her.

"He said you sent him a note, and he was sorry he wasn't awake to see you when you dropped it off."

Natalie gave a sad smile.

"What? What's that about?" Cora asked. "Why are you mopey about it? You like him, he likes you. This is easy math, Nat. Talk to me."

"We agreed that we would never work out," Natalie said. "And that's that. So there's really nothing to talk about." She crossed the room to the staircase, all business. "I'm thinking new carpet. There's a bloodstain on the landing. It isn't big, but I'm just thinking an overall change is needed."

"Natalie…"

"But what do you think about hardwood? Too loud? Will we hear guests stomping up and down the stairs at all hours of the night? Probably. Hmm."

"Natalie…"

"But hardwood would definitely add to the lodgey vibe, don't you think? We could go rustic, with some of those bear statues that are carved out of tree trunks, and lots of evergreen and brick red in the color scheme."

"Natalie!"

She whirled around. "What?"

"It's okay to fall in love. They're not all Jed Grunder. Superman is definitely not Jed."

Natalie felt herself wanting to slump in defeat. She knew it was okay. She knew it. And she knew Gabriel was a wonderful, safe man. But she just couldn't quite get there in her heart. There was vulnerable, and there was *vulnerable*. She'd had enough of one. "Why don't you get some tea going for when Cambria and Heidy get here, and I'll go check on the animals."

Cora offered a thin smile. "If you say so."

"I might spend some time on the ledge, too, so if I'm not back right away, don't freak out."

"I mean, what are the chances an escaped prisoner will sneak in while we're just innocently going about our day?" Cora joked. But Natalie could see the flit of fear cross her eyes. "Yeah, I know. Too soon."

"You need to stop listening to so many true crime podcasts," Natalie said, playing along. She donned her jacket, gloves, hat and scarf, and grabbed some birdseed and a bag full of peanuts for the squirrels.

The sky was clear, brilliantly blue, clouds lazily bobbing while birds swooped and dipped beneath them. The mountain smelled crisp and clean and full of promise. It was the scent that drew her in the first time she came up here. The clarity of the sky that gave her hope.

If only she felt that hope now.

It took a while to get the heated birdbath up and running again and fill all the feeders. She had a nice, long, apologetic conversation with Felix, who angrily nattered at her for not keeping his feeders full.

She heard a rhythmic creak and *thunk* and saw that the lift station door was left open and was banging against the side of the building in the breeze.

"Oh, Jordan," she said by way of habit and then stopped in her tracks, realizing that she was the one who'd left it open this time. And she knew what was likely inside. Someone would have to take care of that. She didn't want to be the one. She didn't even want to look at it, much less sink her hands into a sponge as she wiped it up. But she knew that she needed to be the one. This would not be a job for the new housekeepers, and it would not be a job for poor Jordan. Gabriel's blood was spilled, and she would be the one to take care of it.

But, later. Later.

She closed the door without looking and calmly walked across the run toward the tree line. Her heart wanted to speed up in memory of what had happened here. She found herself searching for clues—footprints, ski ruts, clearings in the snow where Gabriel had tussled with Jed. But time had worn on and the snow had melted away, and it was as if nothing ever happened here. How was that possible?

She pushed through the trees, finding it hard to appreciate them as she used to do. She couldn't concentrate with all the images and memories flowing through her mind. She had half a mind to turn around. To shut down the Hideaway, get in her Jeep and drive away forever.

But she knew it wasn't the Hideaway that gave her bad memories.

She finally found herself coming upon the ledge, and, despite herself, she was a little disappointed to not find Gabriel there, praying, watching the eagles.

The ledge was empty. The sun shone directly on it, making the rock bare and warm. Spring would be coming before she knew it. She lowered herself to the ledge.

...when you're sitting here, it's a whole different feeling. Like you're part of something much, much bigger. Like you don't always have to do the conquering. There's freedom in that.

Henrietta swooped by, and in that moment, Natalie saw her through Gabriel's eyes. Majestic, awe-inspiring.

He came here to pray that day. She came here to pray today.

"Hey, God," she said, feeling a little self-conscious. "Could you maybe like… I don't know…make this easier? Get him out of my head or something? I can't concentrate, I can't think of anything else, and I know I'll never see him again."

She heard a noise behind her. A rustling of leaves being disturbed. She jumped—hard to get out of old fears—and spun around.

Part of her expected to see Gabriel standing there. Just like on the day they met. Only with no storm pushing in. All blue sky and chirping birds and banter. In fact, she expected it so much, at first her brain tricked her into thinking that was exactly what she was seeing.

Eyes. She definitely saw eyes peering through the woods and back at her. But they were low to the ground. Too low to be a man. Too yellow to be human.

She gasped as it sprang quickly out of sight. The mountain lion. Brad? Sure looked like him. She scrambled up into a crouch, ready to move if she had to. Not that she could outrun or out-anything a mountain lion. But that wouldn't stop her from trying.

And this, she'd come to learn, was who she was. Not a woman who was always afraid and running, but a woman who was always prepared to fight for herself. There was a difference.

To her surprise, the mountain lion popped out of the foliage about twenty feet down the mountain, on another ledge just like her own. Too small for a person to sit on, but just perfect for an animal. She watched as the cat sat and looked over the valley, then lowered herself so she was sitting again, too. For a long while, she and the cat scanned the goings-on down below together, feeling the sun on their faces. The cat's eyes began drifting closed, and then it turned and curled up on the ledge, its face pointing toward Natalie.

It was astonishingly beautiful. And it seemed to know things. Maybe it, too, was an overthinker.

"You know," she said, "if he was here, I think I would tell him." The cat blinked but said nothing. "I would. I definitely wouldn't let him slip through my fingers a second time." The cat closed its eyes, sleepy. "Oh, so you disagree? Well, you're wrong. I would tell him. In fact, if he shows up again, I *will* tell him. You'll just have to wait and see."

Natalie had just started to get chilly when she heard the crunch of tires in the parking lot. The new housekeepers had arrived, and surely Cora's tea was ready. It would feel good to wrap her hands around a warm mug.

Her movement woke the cat, which opened one eye, slightly raised its head and then rested its chin back on its paws.

"See you around, Brad," she said, and then turned and made her way back to the lodge.

Gabriel had been waiting for an envelope for weeks now. Or a phone call. Email. Something to let him know that he'd gotten into law school and the rest of his life was starting.

He wished he was as excited as he was supposed to be. He suspected he would be if Natalie was there to hear the news with him. He suspected that about a lot of things—that it would be better with Natalie there. He couldn't seem to get her out of his mind.

Still, even without her, he waited at the mailbox for that acceptance letter every single day.

He walked to the mailbox today, noticing how beautiful and clear the weather was. He bet the ledge he'd fallen in love with up in Bighorn was magical on a day like today. Just like every thought he had these days—even walking to the mailbox somehow came back to Natalie.

He opened the mailbox.

Today, at last, there was an envelope. He ripped it open so fast, he tore the letter inside, too. He forced himself to slow down, unfold; the message inside wasn't going to change, and if he'd waited this long, what was another ten seconds? He was reading before he even had it all the way unfolded.

We are happy to inform you...

He whooped and punched the sky, so elated he could hardly stand it. This was it. This was the rest of his life starting. He laughed, clutched his side, laughed some more, the rest of the mail scattering on the ground.

"Yes!" he cried. "Yes, sir! Whoo-hoo-hoo!"

When he bent to pick up the dropped mail, he noticed a card. Surprisingly, the return address was the Snowed Inn Hideaway. His heart *thunked* hard in his chest. Natalie? Had she found a way to be here with him when he found out after all?

He ripped open the card with almost the same vigor that he'd ripped open the acceptance letter. What timing.

It was an invitation. Not from Natalie, but from Cora. Inviting him to a grand reopening of the Hideaway. She'd written a note at the bottom: *As guest of honor, we would like to treat you to a private dinner before the festivities. Please say you'll come.*

He found himself grinning so hard he could feel it in his ears. He probably looked ridiculous, standing out at the mailbox, smiling, laughing, celebrating all by himself. But he couldn't help it. He pulled his phone out of his back pocket and texted the number written at the bottom of the invitation.

Yes. Yes, of course I'll be there. I wouldn't miss it for anything in the world.

Chapter Seventeen

Cora had pitched the idea of a grand reopening celebration, and Natalie had gotten instantly on board. A celebration to set the tone of the Snowed Inn Hideaway from here on out. They had loads of activities planned. A string quartet, a cupcake tower brought in by a catering company and two men in black vests at the ready with complimentary crudités. They'd brought in horses for mountain riding, and Jordan was there to oversee the skiing. They offered special rates and were completely booked for the first time since that storm drove everyone away months ago.

Tomorrow was the day. Natalie was excited but a little nervous. She'd puttered most of the day away and was ready for the hearty dinner she smelled.

"I've got the fire going," she said, walking into the kitchen. She expected to find Cora there, bustling over who-knew-what. But instead she found herself standing in a darkened room, lit only by candles on a delicately set table. Something bubbled in a pot on the stove, smelling delicious, and a salad bowl was at the ready on the counter. "What is this?"

"Oh, there you are," Cora said, hurrying in behind her. "Good. Go ahead and have a seat. Dinner will be ready any minute."

Natalie laughed. "We're having a romantic dinner for two? Who's going to work the desk?"

"Not *our* dinner, silly. Yours," Cora said. "I'll work the desk. Sit. Sit." She had picked up the salad bowl and was nudging Natalie toward the table with it.

"Okay, okay, but I don't understand."

Her words fell away as a figure filled the doorway, looking shy and uncertain. "Sorry to intrude. I heard voices back here. I…had an invitation?" He awkwardly held up a card.

Natalie couldn't speak. She was certain that the person standing in the kitchen was Gabriel, but it couldn't be.

"Wonderful! You made it!" Cora set the salad bowl back on the counter and rushed to him, arms extended for a huge hug. "You sure are a sight for sore eyes. What do you think of the remodel?"

"It's gorgeous in here," he said, but he looked directly at Natalie while he said it, sending tingles through her. She quickly looked down at her lap. Her mind raced. How was Gabriel here? What had Cora done?

Cora released him from her grip and steered him toward the table. "Have a seat. I was just about to serve the salad."

Gabriel sat, and he and Natalie endured Cora's fussing, exchanging amused looks the entire time.

She piled salad on each of their plates and brought warm bread and butter. It smelled amazing, but Natalie couldn't even think about eating. Not with so many questions flying around in her head. So many thoughts.

So many promises she'd made to an empty sky and a sleeping mountain lion. When Gabriel was away, she was certain she would do anything, say anything to get him back into her life. But now that he was here, she felt shy.

Cora finished up, brushed off her hands, shooed the housekeepers out of the room, and they were finally alone.

"I think we might have been set up. What do you think?" Gabriel asked.

"Cora is very sneaky," Natalie said. "I had no idea."

"I was told I was the guest of honor at a private dinner."

Natalie smiled. "Well. I am quite honored to see you. You look good, by the way. Better than good."

"You, too."

They each took bites of their salad. Natalie chewed but tasted nothing. "So you're healing well?"

"Mostly," he said. "Still a little discomfort here and there. But I'm alive. I think I have you to thank."

"Funny, I think I have you to thank. I wouldn't have made it ten seconds against Jed if you hadn't been here. Cora and I would have both died."

"Sometimes I think I might have been here for a reason," Gabriel said. "I've done a lot of asking myself what that reason was, of course. Why me, and all that."

"Did you ever come up with an answer?"

He shrugged. "Sort of. I think I was meant to meet you. I know that sounds crazy."

"No, it doesn't sound crazy at all. I think so, too," Natalie said.

They went back to their shy eating, Natalie feeling more and more uncomfortable. Not because she felt uncomfortable around Gabriel but because she felt uncomfortable being so far away, even if she was just across the table.

"So I got into law school," he said. "Found out last week."

Natalie's eyes lit up. "You did? Where?"

"University of Wyoming."

"That's wonderful, Gabriel. I was wondering if you'd ever made your decision. I'm so happy for you."

"Thank you. I got some good advice and decided to go for it. Got a long road ahead, but I was offered a job in a law office. Just answering phones and transcribing. Nothing major. But it'll be good experience, and I won't be chasing criminals anymore. I think I've had enough of that. And besides…"

Natalie set down her fork and reached across the table for his hand, interrupting him. "I want to go with you."

Gabriel blinked in surprise, still holding his fork, but all of his attention was focused on her warm hand, and the words he could have sworn he heard her say.

"I'm sorry? What did you…?"

"I want to go with you," she said. "I… This is really hard, Gabriel, but I made a promise to Brad, and I have to live up to that promise."

"Who's Brad?"

"The mountain lion? I told you about him in my note. You got my note, right?"

"Yeah, but…"

"Anyway, I told Brad that if you were up here again, I wouldn't make the mistake of hiding from you again. I would tell you how I felt. So I'm telling you how I feel. I'm in love with you. I've always been in love with you. Probably since that first time I ran into you on the ledge."

"Natalie…"

"No, if I don't say it all now, I'll chicken out, and this is too important to me. I'm scared. Trust and falling in love got me really hurt in the past. I'd walled myself off from ever having that hurt again. But then the hurt came to my doorstep, and it was terrifying, but I had you. And I almost lost you. And the idea of never seeing you again was awful. I realized that real hurt is the hurt of not being with you."

"Natalie…"

"Let me finish. I have to say this. You may not feel the same way. But if you do, that would be amazing, and I'll go to Laramie to be with you."

Gabriel gently pulled his hand out of Natalie's and set down his fork. His heart was nearly bursting with happiness. She was saying all the things he wanted to say to her and was afraid of saying. Could it really, after all this time, be so easy?

Natalie abruptly stopped talking. Her blazing eyes

were wet and swimmy but excited in the candlelight. She was more beautiful than he'd ever seen her. He had a feeling there were a million beautiful faces of Natalie Marlowe, and he'd only seen a handful. That handful could carry him through a lifetime.

"I feel the same way," he said. "I'm so relieved to hear you say this. I'm in love with you, too. And I've been afraid of being hurt again the way Liane hurt me. But keeping you out is worse than losing her ever was. I love you, Natalie. It was first sight."

Natalie let out a breath that was half sob, the glisten in her eyes spilling over onto her cheeks. Yet another beautiful face of Natalie. "Does that mean you won't mind if I go to Laramie, too? I'll get my own place, of course."

"But what about the Hideaway?" he asked.

"I've got a co-owner now. Laramie isn't that far. I'll come up a few times a month. It'll be fine."

"You'd be leaving your dreams to follow mine."

"My dreams aren't dreams without you in them," she said. "None of that matters. We'll work out the details. The important thing is that we're together."

"I couldn't agree more."

Gabriel reached out with his other hand and stood, pulling Natalie out of her seat, too. They stood close, holding hands. He could smell honey-scented lotion on her, and firewood, and soft clothing.

"There's something else I've been wanting to do since we met on that ledge," he said, reaching up to brush a strand of hair from her forehead.

"Me, too," Natalie breathed.

Gabriel leaned in and kissed her, soft and sweet and perfect. He felt the pieces of his life clicking together, a puzzle assembling itself. He never thought he could feel so happy. He pulled her in for an embrace. "You know what this feels like?"

"Like flying?" she said into his shoulder.

He smiled. "Yeah. Like that. It feels exactly like flying."

He tilted her face up and leaned down for another kiss, their hearts beating together like the rhythmic flap of an eagle's wings.

* * * * *

Get 3 FREE REWARDS!

We'll send you 2 FREE Books plus a FREE Mystery Gift.

FREE Value Over **$20**

Both the **Love Inspired®** and **Love Inspired® Suspense** series feature compelling novels filled with inspirational romance, faith, forgiveness and hope.

YES! Please send me 2 FREE novels from the Love Inspired or Love Inspired Suspense series and my FREE gift (gift is worth about $10 retail). After receiving them, if I don't wish to receive any more books, I can return the shipping statement marked "cancel." If I don't cancel, I will receive 6 brand-new Love Inspired Larger-Print books or Love Inspired Suspense Larger-Print books every month and be billed just $6.49 each in the U.S. or $6.74 each in Canada. That is a savings of at least 16% off the cover price. It's quite a bargain! Shipping and handling is just 50¢ per book in the U.S. and $1.25 per book in Canada.* I understand that accepting the 2 free books and gift places me under no obligation to buy anything. I can always return a shipment and cancel at any time by calling the number below. The free books and gift are mine to keep no matter what I decide.

Choose one:
- ☐ **Love Inspired Larger-Print** (122/322 BPA GRPA)
- ☐ **Love Inspired Suspense Larger-Print** (107/307 BPA GRPA)
- ☐ **Or Try Both!** (122/322 & 107/307 BPA GRRP)

Name (please print)

Address   Apt. #

City   State/Province   Zip/Postal Code

Email: Please check this box ☐ if you would like to receive newsletters and promotional emails from Harlequin Enterprises ULC and its affiliates. You can unsubscribe anytime.

Mail to the Harlequin Reader Service:
IN U.S.A.: P.O. Box 1341, Buffalo, NY 14240-8531
IN CANADA: P.O. Box 603, Fort Erie, Ontario L2A 5X3

Want to try 2 free books from another series! Call 1-800-873-8635 or visit www.ReaderService.com.

*Terms and prices subject to change without notice. Prices do not include sales taxes, which will be charged (if applicable) based on your state or country of residence. Canadian residents will be charged applicable taxes. Offer not valid in Quebec. This offer is limited to one order per household. Books received may not be as shown. Not valid for current subscribers to the Love Inspired or Love Inspired Suspense series. All orders subject to approval. Credit or debit balances in a customer's account(s) may be offset by any other outstanding balance owed by or to the customer. Please allow 4 to 6 weeks for delivery. Offer available while quantities last.

Your Privacy—Your information is being collected by Harlequin Enterprises ULC, operating as Harlequin Reader Service. For a complete summary of the information we collect, how we use this information and to whom it is disclosed, please visit our privacy notice located at corporate.harlequin.com/privacy-notice. From time to time we may also exchange your personal information with reputable third parties. If you wish to opt out of this sharing of your personal information, please visit readerservice.com/consumerchoice or call 1-800-873-8635. **Notice to California Residents**—Under California law, you have specific rights to control and access your data. For more information on these rights and how to exercise them, visit corporate.harlequin.com/california-privacy.

LIRLIS23

Get 3 FREE REWARDS!

We'll send you 2 FREE Books _plus_ a FREE Mystery Gift.

FREE Value Over **$20**

Both the **Harlequin® Special Edition** and **Harlequin® Heartwarming™** series feature compelling novels filled with stories of love and strength where the bonds of friendship, family and community unite.

YES! Please send me 2 FREE novels from the Harlequin Special Edition or Harlequin Heartwarming series and my FREE Gift (gift is worth about $10 retail). After receiving them, if I don't wish to receive any more books, I can return the shipping statement marked "cancel." If I don't cancel, I will receive 6 brand-new Harlequin Special Edition books every month and be billed just $5.49 each in the U.S. or $6.24 each in Canada, a savings of at least 12% off the cover price, or 4 brand-new Harlequin Heartwarming Larger-Print books every month and be billed just $6.24 each in the U.S. or $6.74 each in Canada, a savings of at least 19% off the cover price. It's quite a bargain! Shipping and handling is just 50¢ per book in the U.S. and $1.25 per book in Canada.* I understand that accepting the 2 free books and gift places me under no obligation to buy anything. I can always return a shipment and cancel at any time by calling the number below. The free books and gift are mine to keep no matter what I decide.

Choose one: ☐ **Harlequin Special Edition** (235/335 BPA GRMK)   ☐ **Harlequin Heartwarming Larger-Print** (161/361 BPA GRMK)   ☐ **Or Try Both!** (235/335 & 161/361 BPA GRPZ)

Name (please print)

Address   Apt. #

City   State/Province   Zip/Postal Code

Email: Please check this box ☐ if you would like to receive newsletters and promotional emails from Harlequin Enterprises ULC and its affiliates. You can unsubscribe anytime.

Mail to the Harlequin Reader Service:
IN U.S.A.: P.O. Box 1341, Buffalo, NY 14240-8531
IN CANADA: P.O. Box 603, Fort Erie, Ontario L2A 5X3

Want to try 2 free books from another series! Call 1-800-873-8635 or visit www.ReaderService.com.

HARLEQUIN
PLUS

Try the best multimedia subscription service for romance readers like you!

Read, Watch and Play.

Experience the easiest way to get the romance content you crave.

Start your **FREE TRIAL** at
<u>www.harlequinplus.com/freetrial</u>.